Old M Hubby

JAMILA JASPER

JAMILA JASPER

ISBN: 9781520152219

DEDICATION

To my greatest love.

JAMILA JASPER

CONTENTS

ACKNOWLEDGMENTS

Thank you K. You've never let me down yet!

1 THIRD IN LINE

Alana Morris woke up to a series of sweet good-night text messages from Paul. After a late night babysitting shift, Alana had crashed before they had a chance to talk. Alana struggled to find time to talk to Paul these days. With graduate school piling on the pressure and her work commitments getting greater, Alana wasn't sure how she found time for this new relationship.

She got out of bed and checked her calendar. Three days until her period. Ugh. That explained that gross, bloated feeling that was gnawing at her gut. Alana began her morning ritual. She washed her face, brushed her teeth and then hopped into the shower. She co-washed her waist length natural hair, finger-detangling the thick black coils.

After her shower, Alana wrapped her hair up in a t-shirt to dry and slipped into a white button up blouse, dark wash jeans and brown boots. The boots had been a recent gift from Paul; Alana had never owned a pair of boots so expensive before but Paul had handed the gift to her like it was nothing.

Alana didn't know what to make of her new boyfriend sometimes. He was everything she could have dreamed of in a man — and more. But they couldn't have been more different or come from more different backgrounds.

Alana was twenty-six years old and she'd been the first in her family to go to college. She'd graduated from the University of Georgia with a degree in psychology and moved on to graduate school after working at a local psychiatric hospital for a year. Alana's entire life was driven by the imperative to survive. She was the pride and joy of the Morris family and she hadn't crumbled under the pressure.

Alana had dark, sepia-toned skin with copper undertones. She'd "gone natural" during undergrad and the results of that were only now visible with her waist length natural hair. She had a nose piercing, wore diamonds in her ears, had a small tattoo of a butterfly above her left hip and stood at average height. Alana might have been average in a few ways but certainly not when it came to looks or intellect — two areas she excelled in.

At twenty-six years old, everyone in her family had supported Alana's initiative to go to grad school, some of them had even raised money for Alana's tuition. She had a horde of people she couldn't bear to disappoint. Despite the fact that she'd made it to grad school, survival was still just out of reach for Alana. Her grad school stipend barely covered rent and books. She still had to eat, buy clothing, pay her student loan bills from her undergraduate degree and save money.

So unlike most of the students in Alana's program who came from money, Alana worked as much as possible. Not many jobs could fit in with her hours so she'd worked a couple night shifts at the university café, she babysat for friends and she edited students' papers. Alana was busy...

Almost too busy for a boyfriend.

A boyfriend like Paul seemed to require an empty schedule that Alana didn't have. Paul wasn't just Paul. He was Paul Quincy Hanover III. He'd come from a long line of wealthy men. He had that old Southern money, so old that it was taboo to talk about where it came from. He'd gone to two of the finest boarding schools in the United States and University of Virginia for undergrad.

Paul was attending Alana's university now to get an MBA — but he didn't seem to need it. He knew that he was going to inherit his daddy's insurance company up North and he was getting the MBA just to satisfy his family. Paul's attitude towards his education differed from Alana's entirely.

To him, this was a hobby, something to pass the time. To Alana, her graduate degree was everything. She'd been working towards making the Morris family proud her whole life and she didn't know how to do anything else. Paul simply didn't have that kind of pressure. He was set for life and he'd always had been.

In their five months of dating, Alana had a hard time getting much information out of Paul about his finances. She could tell they were in very very good condition. Paul bought her Tiffany's jewelry, nice watches, nice purses and took her on incredible weekends in Palm Springs. By helicopter.

Alana was head over heels in love with Paul but still hesitant about their relationship. She hadn't said "I love you" to Paul and they hadn't even slept together. Alana was accustomed to allowing her impulses to take the lead when it came to men. She was the type to fall in love after three dates and fall into bed with a man soon after. After three too many heartbreaks, Alana had decided to take things nice and slow with Paul Quincy Hanover III.

With Paul, Alana experienced something she never had with men before. She was suspicious. It was strange for her to admit to herself but it was the truth. Paul came from a long line of Southern folks. Those types of folks "Southern hospitality" didn't usually extend to women of a certain hue.

But Alana had never detected anything "off" about Paul. He didn't seem to care what her skin color was. He didn't care what looks they attracted hanging around Palm Springs or sitting in upscale restaurants. Paul seemed to be smitten with Alana as a person. He loved that she could recite Langston Hughes poetry and that her favorite author was Toni Morrison. He loved that Alana could talk his ear off about jazz from Ma Rainey to Billie Holiday.

So, given that Paul seemed so normal, Alana was on the verge of letting her guard down. Alana ran some coconut oil, then Shea butter through her hair and then braided two thick cornrows down the sides of her head. Alana wasn't one for much makeup in the heat of the sun. But with summer approaching, she felt a bit on the festive side. Alana colored her lips in a deep mulberry lipstick and curled her eyelashes.

Perfect.

That way, even if she ran into Paul unexpectedly, she'd look effortlessly beautiful.

Before heading out of the house, Alana's phone rang. Desiree. Desiree was an older friend of Alana's that she'd met by hap and stance while shopping one day. Desiree seemed desperate for a younger woman to dole out unsolicited advice to and Alana had fit the bill perfectly.

"Alana? Is that you?"

"Yes it's me. Do you need me to clip a credit card again?"

Desiree laughed, "No doll don't worry about me. I have things *all* under control. I was wondering actually… I've got this friend named Jada who needs a babysitter… Are you free Friday night?"

"Yes!" Alana said without checking her schedule.

"That'll be fifty dollars an hour though."

"Oh honey Jada ain't got an issue with that."

Alana silently thanked the heavens that she'd managed to land a new client so easily. She was starting to run short on cash and she didn't relish the idea of her current last ditch solution — asking Paul for a small loan.

"Perfect then. Just give her my number and I'll see what I can do."

"You okay otherwise?" Desiree asked.

Desiree seemed to have this uncanny ability to read other's emotions with ease. She could always tell when something was wrong with Alana — especially if it was in the romance department.

"Well, I have to see Paul soon and I'm going *nuts* just thinking about it."

"Paul? Rich Paul?"

Alana rolled her eyes, glad that Desiree couldn't see. Desiree seemed to analyze men by their wallets first, their looks second and their personalities not at all. Alana kept it to herself but she was convinced that Desiree's materialism had ended her marriage.

"Yes, rich Paul."

"What's the problem? Is he one of those stingy guys?"

"No it's not that. He's great. It's just… I worry that I'm being naive about this. He's in line to inherit a massive family fortune and I'm just Alana Morris. And I'm *black.*"

"So what? White boys love 'em some brown sugar in the South. There's nothing new about that."

Alana wasn't sure she was getting through to Desiree the way she wanted to. She wasn't sure that Desiree could even understand the fact that she didn't want to be some white man's dirty little secret. She wasn't looking for a sugar daddy or a salacious affair. Alana was looking for the real thing.

"I want to get married Desiree. I don't just want some guy to treat me like his plaything."

Desiree clicked her teeth, "Oh to be young… Listen dear, I'm glad you can do some babysitting for my friend. When it comes to Paul, just make sure he doesn't have any creepy skeletons in his closet and you'll be fine. Stop worrying. And don't do anything impulsive."

"Okay."

"Toodles! I'm headed out shopping and I'll see if I can get you a little something."

Desiree's idea of a "little something" was entirely different from Alana's. Desiree was a confusing, complicated woman who used her materialism to cover up a lifetime of deep hurt and rejection. Alana didn't fall for her charade and saw the kind, generous woman who masked herself in wigs, inches of makeup and Versace. Desiree always had Alana's back. Since she'd started grad school, Alana had hardly needed to worry about clothes. She'd get a few of Desiree's hand-me-downs and sell them.

Usually, one of Desiree's outfits could be re-sold for $2,000. With that money, Alana would toss some into her savings account and buy new clothes from Target with the rest. Desiree was none the wiser. For all her struggling, Alana knew how to make a dollar stretch in a pinch.

As Alana walked to the bus stop, she looked at pictures of Paul and herself that were stored in her phone. They *did* look happy together. They really did.

Alana remembered the first time she'd met Paul. She was studying in the university library when he was sitting with a few of his MBA friends. They were watching something and guffawing at the top of their lungs. Alana glanced over a few times and caught Paul's eye. He seemed to be the ring-leader of the little group. Still, despite her dirty looks, Paul and his gang continued to laugh at the top of their lungs.

Alana had set her books to the side and marched over there, asking them in a less than kind tone to please quiet down and stop acting like a bunch of "undergraduate hooligans" in the library. The entire time, Paul had this shit-eating grin plastered across his face that she'd found entirely annoying... and sexy.

She had returned to her seat musing about how such an attractive guy could be so inconsiderate. She'd been sitting down for no more than five minutes when Paul had run up to her table and asked her out on a date. Alana had balked at his suggestion at first — wondering what she could *possibly* have had in common with him. Paul had begged and stated his case until Alana gave in.

What could be the harm? Paul had promised to pay and he'd promised to make the date worth her time.

He'd delivered on his promise. After a fabulous dinner, Paul had taken her on a walk along a secluded nature trail. In the woods, everything was quiet except the loud vibrant buzz of cicadas and crickets. The smell of magnolias waned as autumn was starting to set in. Then, right as they'd reached a well lit pond area, Paul had kissed her and told her that she was the most beautiful woman he'd ever met.

From that day on, Alana was smitten.

Paul wasn't hard on the eyes either. He towered over her at six-foot-four and he had the physique of a football player with strong broad shoulders and a nice meaty buttocks. He had deep tanned skin from hours of sailing and tennis. His hair was an ash brown color that was almost bleached blonde at the top. His eyes were a pretty cornflower blue that reminded Alana of summer. And of course there was his smile…

Paul's impish smile could light up Alana's entire day. And since their first date, she'd lived to see a grin break out across his face. Paul had been an amazing lover. He'd been patient with Alana's desire to abstain from anything intimate and he'd spoiled and pampered her every single day he'd known her.

Alana knew they were an unlikely pair. She was an introverted bookworm who divided her time between work and the library. Paul was an outgoing party animal who knew any and everybody in their grad program. He was the guy who rented out swanky venues to throw over-the-top parties. He went on vacations to the Bahamas with fourteen of his closest friends. Alana knew his socializing made him well-suited for business. Plus, opposites tended to attract.

She loved how Paul could go on and on for hours about all the subjects he was interested in. He loved that Alana was a patient listener who never seemed to grow weary of his antics. Alana couldn't wait for them to have been together for a year. She yearned to tell Paul the truth about how she felt for him — to tell him that she *loved* him, but she was still hesitant.

Alana had been burned so many times in the past that when things finally felt right, she hesitated.

The bus stopped at the library and Alana hiked her tote bag further up her shoulder as she entered the giant building and swiped her card through the sensors. It was Sunday morning at eight and there was no way in hell she'd find Paul here. Or anyone really. This was Alana's special time. She could get most of her reading done for the week while tucked into a quiet corner and she wouldn't miss a thing. She knew her mama would be *furious* if she knew what her daughter was doing on the Lord's day. But Alana was too busy with school and work and her new relationship to make any other time…

She started reading in the corner of the library until her eyelids grew heavy. Alana was almost through with her thesis but certain aspects of it still required her to read until her mind was numb. As the complex psychological terms and analysis floated into her brain, Alana started to feel more at ease. Answers jumped out at her, as did more questions. She relaxed into her work and didn't look up to check the time until it was almost noon.

By noon, Alana turned on her cellphone and reconnected with the outside world. She had three missed calls from Paul. Alana rolled her eyes. She loved him, but for some reason Paul couldn't get the message that she *worked* all of Sunday morning. She was sure that he was ardently concerned about her whereabouts to the point of frenetic.

Since it was close to lunch time anyway, Alana packed up her books and walked outside. The afternoon sun was warming up. She returned Paul's phone call.

"Hey stranger," He answered.

"Sorry, I've been studying."

Paul chuckled, "You're always studying. Well I'm studying myself… Studying how to get over a massive hangover. What are you up to tonight? I want to take you out."

"Tonight? More studying!"

Paul laughed.

"Come on Paul! We're in grad school! Don't you think you should be studying too?"

"Don't need to study."

"OK Mr. Genius."

"Hey, don't get testy missy. I know you're just tired 'cause you haven't seen a damn thing that's not a library book in the past few days."

"Well…"

He wasn't wrong. Still, Alana had very important reasons for keeping herself cooped up in the library. She was trying to graduate with a distinction and she didn't keep her grades up by leaving her post every time Paul decided they needed to spend more time together.

"Don't be suck a stick in the mud. You know I'll take care of you Alana…"

"So what? That means I never work again?"

"Maybe," Paul replied cheekily.

"You're something else, you know that?"

"Is that a yes?"

"I *might* be able to do dinner at seven thirty."

"How about seven?"

"Fine," Alana sighed, "I think I can work with seven o'clock."

"Perfect. You won't regret it."

"Let's hope my transcript feels the same way," Alana grumbled.
"Relax Alana… When have you *ever* had a bad date with me?"

Paul was right. Every moment she'd spent with him had been exhilarating. Alana was actually close to the point where she was ready to "do it" with him. After months of dating, and months of everything feeling almost ethereal, her emotions were in the right place. Despite her lingering doubts about their future, Alana at least didn't doubt that Paul's feelings for her were present and strong.

"I'll be ready by seven."

"I'll come pick you up then. Wear something low cut."

"Paul!"

"Sorry, couldn't help myself. It was at least worth the try, right?"

"I can't handle your mischief, you know that?"

Paul laughed, "Oh baby… I think you can."

"Goodbye Paul."

"See you later darling."

When Alana hung up her chest was bursting with excitement. Even if Paul never seemed to understand her passion for working 24/7, he at least understood how to treat her. If Paul promised her an amazing night, Alana was absolutely certain he would deliver. Unfortunately, she only had seven hours left to plan out her schedule for the next week, confirm her babysitting commitments and then finish up her readings for her classes.

Alana walked to the bus stop to catch a ride to her favorite café. On Sundays when she had a lot to do, she'd order a triple shot of espresso over ice and pop on some hip-hop instrumentals. That always got the job done. At first the servers at the café had given her a look when she was crazy, but Alana swore by that drink like some of her classmates swore by Ritalin. At least there was nothing illegal about espresso.

After hours at the café, Alana found herself ahead of schedule. Desiree's friend had called her and confirmed a big babysitting job where she could plan to net $500 in a weekend. It wasn't a bad deal except for the fact that Desiree's friend had four kids and a baby. Alana had her work cut out for her.

Alana walked home ninety minutes before she was supposed to have dinner with Paul. Once she was home, she wrapped her hair up in a shower cap and took a nice long, hot shower. All the stress from her long day of reading and note-taking melted away under the soothing head of her shower. Once she'd dried off and applied cocoa butter to every inch of her skin, Alana had to choose an outfit.

With Paul, she could never tell what an appropriate outfit for a night out might be. That was a part of the fun of course — he could take her to a five star restaurant or walking down a woodsy path filled with beautiful wildflowers — but before her dates, Alana always felt a bit stressed.

She opted for something simple. She threw on a knee-length black dress and wore the pearls that Paul had got for her birthday around her neck. After only three months of dating he'd bought her a string of classic Mikimoto pearls. At first Alana had been almost *terrified* to wear anything quite so luxurious. But Paul seemed to love the way the glistening objects draped around her sepia colored neck.

Again, Alana didn't wear much makeup. She hated the sticky feeling on her face in the Southern heat. Just when she was ready, she heard Paul's car pull up outside.

He never allowed Alana to walk to his car alone. Whether it was some notion of chivalry or just common decency, Paul always knocked on Alana's door and politely linked arms with her as he led her to his brand new C-class Mercedes. Alana met Paul in the lobby of her studio apartment. He embraced her and kissed her on the cheek.

"You look amazing… And you smell good too. What perfume are you wearing?"

Alana lowered her eyes shyly, "No perfume. Just cocoa butter."

"Cocoa butter?'

Alana giggled. In some ways, Paul's ignorance about everything that was *normal* to her was funny. She held onto his arm and said, "You'll have to try some next time you come over to my place."

Paul nodded. They made their way to his car and he held open the car door while Alana slipped into the passenger seat. Paul revved up the engine and started driving towards their mystery date destination.

"Sure thing. How was your day of studying darling? I missed you today."

"But clearly you didn't miss me last night when you were getting that hangover," She teased.

"Oh that was just a night out with the guys. Biff's girl dumped him so we got him wasted and I played wingman for the night."

"Any luck?"

"Hell no. The only thing Biff's got going for him is his money. He shouldn't have messed around on Angie or he wouldn't have been in this position."

Paul seemed to want to change the subject, "So, how was your day?"

Alana shrugged, "Nothing special. Worked in the library then went over to the café. I got a new babysitting gig!"

"Incredible. Does it pay alright?"

Alana nodded, "The pay's great and it's for a mutual friend so I'm sure it won't be too difficult."

"Perfect…"

Paul turned his car 'round a corner and approached a posh looking restaurant with a giant gilded sign above it that said, "The Lodge".

"The Lodge?!" Alana gasped.

"Yup. I figured it's about time we go here…"

The Lodge was one of those just out of town restaurants that women at Alana's university bragged about going to. Most guys took a girl here when they were about to propose to her or when they'd screwed up and needed to apologize in a *big* way. Alana wondered if she was about to get more than she bargained for here.

"Why now?"

"You've been working hard all day. I can't wait 'til the day I can finally take care of you."

Alana pursed her lips. She appreciated the sentiment but a part of her hated the fact that Paul talked about "taking care of her". Alana didn't expect a man to take care of her and she didn't want to send Paul the message that her life plan was to pretend to care about work until she managed to get a ring on her finger. Alana wanted more out of her life than that.

They sat down to dinner and Alana couldn't stop ogling Paul the entire time. He was *gorgeous*. He started talking to her about his recent MBA project and the business mixer he'd have to attend in Miami soon. The restaurant was perfect. Kind waitresses served them up delicious salmon platters and when Alana started eating she was in heaven.

"Like the salmon?"

"I *love* the salmon."

"I could tell you needed a treat like this," Paul started, "You work too damned hard. You deserve to just… relax."

Alana shrugged, "I wish I could relax more. It's just everything's so crazy and I'm trying to graduate with a distinction too —."

"You're high strung," Paul interrupted.

"I have a lot riding on me."

"Too much. What would it take to get a girl like you to unwind a bit?"

Alana wasn't sure if Paul was asking her a serious question. Unwind? She'd be able to unwind once she graduated with a distinction, found a high paying job, helped her mama move into a better apartment, settled down, had kids, then retired. Alana didn't see "unwinding" in her future until she was at least fifty-five.

 "Accomplish all my goals," Alana replied.

Paul chuckled, "Maybe one day… We can make things official and you can learn a little bit about taking it easy."

Alana wasn't sure that day would really ever come.

"Let's just enjoy dinner okay? And maybe afterwards, we can "unwind" at your place."

Paul raised his eyebrows. After Alana had remained so tacitly uninterested in intimacy of any kind, he was surprised that she'd sprung this on him all of a sudden.

"You serious Alana? You know I'm okay with waiting as long as you want to…"

"No. I'm serious. I know what I want Paul… And it's you."

Paul grinned, "Well shucks ain't I a lucky guy."

After dinner, Alana suddenly felt nervous. It wasn't like she'd never been intimate with anyone before. It's just that with Paul, it felt special. So Alana felt this indescribable pressure to perform — this indescribable pressure for everything to be perfect. Paul held the door open as Alana got into the passenger seat again.

On the drive home, Paul kept the conversation light. But Alana could tell he was preoccupied. Paul's left hand was on the steering wheel but his right hand gripped Alana's thighs. She could feel Paul's arousal mounting — as was hers. Alana had spent many nights at Paul's apartment but all those nights she'd slept in the guest bedroom.

Once they pulled into his garage, Paul leaned over and kissed Alana on the lips again.

"You can back out of this any time," Paul whispered.

"I know… But I don't want to back out…"

Paul couldn't have hopped out of his car faster. Before Alana knew it, she was standing in the foyer of Paul's house and his arms were wrapped around her. Alana pressed her lips to his and felt electricity surging through her body. Kissing Paul was always amazing but this time surpassed her expectations. Alana felt moistness pooling between her thighs as Paul's strong hands gripped her hips tightly. He pulled her closer and held her tightly so she couldn't move or break free. All she could do was allow Paul to kiss her.

When Paul's lips finally broke away from hers, Alana was dizzy with glee. Paul held her hand and started to lead her upstairs. Once they were upstairs, Alana started to feel more confidence. She wondered why she'd ever doubted Paul in the first place — why she'd ever wondered about the future of their relationship.

Paul started stripping off Alana's clothing slowly. He revealed her lacy bra and underwear with a few swift motions. As Alana's skin became exposed to the cool air of Paul's bedroom, gooseflesh prickled all over her skin. Paul's lips pressed against her shoulder and then he reached down towards the back of Alana's bra and unhooked her bra. Alana's breasts swung into view. Paul bent his head down and took one of Alana's nipples into his mouth.

Alana let out an unwilling moan as Paul's warm tongue flicked across her hardened, dark nipples. She enjoyed how he took his time with her and was taking his time to warm her up and prepare her for the action. Alana held onto Paul's hair and brought his face up to hers again. Alana kissed Paul and he shoved his tongue into her mouth, preparing her for the ardent thrusting that was soon to follow.

Paul lifted Alana off the ground, ignoring her squeals as he took her over to his bed. As Paul lay her down on her back, Alana gazed into his eyes. Paul's cornflower blue eyes were fixated on her body; he had the gaze of a predator about to chase down his prey. He was eager and desperate for whatever lay between Alana's legs. Paul slipped off Alana's lacy underwear and revealed her exposed pussy.

Alana kept her area neatly trimmed. Once Paul saw her bare pussy, he couldn't resist. There was no more time for foreplay as far as he was concerned. They'd both waited too long for this very moment. Alana spread her legs and Paul stripped down to nothing. Once Alana saw his abs and biceps flexing in the dim light of his bedroom, her pussy surged with anticipation yet again.

"You look *so* hot right now," Paul grunted.

Alana reached her hand down between her legs and started rubbing her engorged clit to entice Paul to hurry and get over here with his big, hard, dick. Paul slid a rubber over his hardness and began to position himself between Alana's legs. As he drew closer, Alana saw Paul's hardness for the first time. He was big… Not just big in fact, *huge*. Alana gasped as she saw what Paul was packing. He had to be over eight inches long with a dick as thick as a coke bottle. She had no clue how she would manage to fit that thing between her legs especially after so many months of celibacy.

"Be gentle," She warned.

"Gentle?" Paul replied with a tone that suggested he would be anything but gentle.

Paul started to insert his dick between Alana's legs. Alana groaned as Paul's massive member started to stretch out her eager wetness. As he thrust those first inches in, she felt indescribable pleasure surging through her body. Alana gasped as Paul started to plunge into her with immense force.

"Ohhh," Alana moaned.

She could feel a climax mounting as pleasure grew and grew between her thighs. Paul pinned her arms above her head and continued to thrust into her. Alana moaned and cried out as she reached her climax...

Paul kept pounding into her wetness, eagerly thrusting until he couldn't anymore. When Paul finally released, Alana shuddered and quivered with pleasure. It felt good to allow him inside her. Paul pulled out and rolled onto his back immediately. Their first romp had been more incredible than Alana had even expected.

In that moment, she knew without a doubt that Paul was the one. Her doubts subsided as she realized once and for all that Paul was the man she wanted to marry and spend the rest of her life with.

2 VINEYARD SUMMERS

The next morning, when Alana woke up in Paul's arms, bliss overwhelmed her. She was nude, enjoying the luxury fabrics rubbing up against her skin. On Mondays, she only had one afternoon class, then babysitting for a few hours. But her mornings were completely clear. Alana couldn't wait until summer when the only thing she'd need to worry about was hustling…

Paul roused himself a few moments after her. Alana could feel his warm arms and warm stomach rubbing against her exposed back as he slowly wriggled awake. Early in the morning, Paul usually had a *rambunctious* appetite for love-making. Alana was eager for him to treat her to a morning romp.

Paul raised his head from bed slowly. His brownish blonde hair was tussled and his blue eyes had a hazy, sleepy look to them.

"Good morning," He mumbled.

"Hey sleepyhead…"

"Mmmph… Coffee…" Paul grumbled.

"Did you program your Keurig?" Alana asked.

Paul replied with a sleepy nod and Alana walked downstairs to grab the cups of coffee that had been made automatically. At least Paul shared her love of routine in some respects. At six in the morning — like clockwork — his coffee maker brewed steaming hot cups of Arabica dark roast. Paul took his coffee with a heaping spoonful of coffee creamer and a dollop of brown sugar. Alana stirred those ingredients into his coffee and brought them upstairs.

Paul had just barely moved. He sat up in bed with a pillow propping up his back. When Alana walked in, the first thing she noticed was Paul's incredible chest and abs. He looked perfect first thing in the morning.

"Mm, that smells good," He muttered as Alana set the coffee on his bedside table.

She joined him in bed and took a sip of her black coffee.

"You're right. It is good."

"My mom sent that down for me. I'm shocked. Usually she has no clue what I like."

"So, what do you have planned today?" Alana asked.

Paul shrugged, "Not much… But I do have something special for you this morning."

"Something special?"

"Yup. I picked out a nice little gift for you that I think you'll love.

Alana waited for him to make a bigger dent in his coffee. Paul kept sipping until it was gone. By the time he'd finished his cup he seemed to have found the energy to give Alana the present he'd promised. Paul walked into his closet and rifled around for a bit before emerging with a slim black box.

Jewelry?

He handed the box to Alana. She tentatively hovered her hand over the cover.

"Open it."

When Alana opened the box she gasped.

"Paul!" She cried out.

"Do you like it?"

Like it? Paul had just handed her a Cartier bracelet. 18-karat white gold with her name engraved into it. Alana. The bracelet had a bright pink gem on both sides of her name.

"Those are sapphires," Paul added when he saw Alana analyzes the entire thing.

"Need help putting it on?"

"I'm almost scared to wear it!"

"Don't be silly Alana… Hold out your wrist."

Paul sat on the bed and held onto Alana's outstretched hand. He kissed her brown, dainty hand and then clasped the bracelet around her wrist. Alana felt like royalty.

"Listen Alana, I'm giving this to you because I want to assure you that we're on the same page here. We both want the same things, right?"

"I want to be with you Paul…"

"And I want to be with you. So I guess I'll have to admit that I have a little bit of an ulterior motive here."

Alana wondered what kind of motive needed to be paid for with a Cartier bracelet. She hoped that Paul hadn't gotten any crazy ideas about threesomes from his friends or something...

"Motive?"

Paul nodded.

"We're both graduating soon and this summer I want you to come up North with me."

"For how long?"

"For the whole summer... As long as you want... Whatever."

"I don't know Paul," Alana said looking down, "I've got a lot of work to do, loans to pay off... I don't know how much time I can spare to go up North."

Paul grinned — Alana could tell by the determined look on his face that he was about to convince her to get rid of any quaint notions about working throughout the summer.

"Listen, my family owns a place up on Martha's Vineyard. You don't have to worry about paying for anything. It's all going to be bankrolled by Paul Hanover II."

"I don't know…"

"Okay then, what's the problem?"

Alana could tell they were quickly descending into the territory where they usually ran into problems. Paul never seemed to understand Alana's drive to take care of herself and forge forth working hard for independence. He might have been happy to take care of her but Alana didn't know how to accept such generosity. Throwing away money like it was nothing just wasn't a part of her worldly experience…

"I just don't know if I can accept that much generosity from your family! I don't want to be anyone's ward."

"You won't be anyone's ward Alana. Come on… You're my girl…"

"I know… But somehow I have to keep my rent paid throughout the summer."

Paul kissed Alana on the forehead. He could tell that Alana was worried. He could tell that somehow, something about his attempts to take care of her made her uncomfortable. Paul didn't understand Alana entirely but he at least tried to comfort her.

"Listen Alana. I wouldn't tell you that I'd take care of it unless we could. Someday, I'm hoping you'll be a part of my family. Us Hanovers take care of each other."

"You're talking about a lot of money though Paul. It's not exactly cheap to fly all the way to Martha's Vineyard! I'm not even fully sure where that is. Maine?"

Paul chuckled, "It's in Massachusetts. But please Alana... I don't want you to worry. I just want you to relax... What can I do to help you relax..."

"Promise me if I come it won't be weird. Promise me no one's going to look at me like the poor Southern black girl who doesn't belong."

Paul shrugged, "Okay fine. I promise."

"Promise?"

"Yes..." He kissed her forehead again.

With that kiss, Alana could feel Paul's love. They still hadn't said those three little words to each other but Alana could sense it in everything that Paul did for her.

"Well I love the bracelet Paul."

"Good… Just promise me you'll come to the Vineyard with me?"

Alana sighed, "Fine… I promise. But if anything goes wrong… I'm blaming you."

"Well I promise… Nothing is going to go wrong. You'll love it. It's nothing like Georgia."

"I hope you're right."

"How about I take your mind off of worrying about things for a bit…" Paul asked.

Alana could tell that he was just trying to get her mind off the subject so she wouldn't change her mind again. The change of pace didn't bug her.

"You can try…" She said impishly.

Paul gently pushed Alana back onto the pillow and stripped the sheets off her legs, exposing her thighs to the cool air of his bedroom.

As Alana lay back in bed, Paul eased between her legs. He pulled off Alana's shorts and exposed her pussy. Alana couldn't wait for Paul to "take her mind off things". They had only made love for the first time and she'd never experienced what Paul was capable of between her legs.

"Last night was incredible," Paul started, "But I can show you a big wide world of pleasure…"

"You can?"

Alana was nervous. At twenty-six, she'd slept with men before, but she'd never had a man put his tongue between her legs. Most of Alana's girl friends thought she was crazy. But most of the men Alana encountered simply didn't care to pleasure her that way. They were more of the type to finish after five or ten minutes and leave her hanging.

"Just relax…"

Alana found it hard to relax. Paul's fingers spread apart her pussy lips and she grew more tense with uncertainty.

"Relax…" He whispered again.

His voice was starting to sound hypnotic and Alana tried to release some of the tension in her body.

"Relax…"

She closed her eyes and waited until Paul's tongue darted between her pussy folds. Alana shuddered as he pried her pussy lips apart a second time and then started pressing his flattened tongue against her engorged wetness. Alana gasped as Paul picked up the pace. His tongue flicked across her clit and Alana quivered in pleasure.

Incredible warmth started to build in her core as she felt Paul feasting furiously on the wetness between her thighs. Paul started to nibble at her labia tenderly while swirling his tongue around her pussy lips swollen with pleasure. Alana was desperate for him to stretch her out again. She reached her hand down and took a thick tuft of his hair in her hands, grinding his face between her thighs.

Paul began to lap at her pussy more furiously. Alana bucked her hips up to meet his eager tongue. She could feel small surges of pleasure building around her clit, assuring her that an immense climax would soon follow. The smell of Paul's animalistic pheromones wafted into Alana's nose driving her even wilder.

There was something about Paul's scent combined with his position between her legs that was driving her wild with anticipation. Alana started to moan softly and as Paul continued to pleasure her, those moans grew louder and louder.

Soon, Alana lost control of herself.

"YES! YES! YES!" She cried out as a climax washed over her body. This was unlike anything she'd ever experienced before.

Paul pressed her hips into the bed, restricting her movement so he could continue his work between her thighs. Her pussy and thighs were damp and covered with a mixture of Paul's saliva and her sweet juices. Alana heaved and gasped for breath as Paul's furious licks didn't let up. He never tired of tasting her; he delivered the exact pleasure he'd promised.

Alana could feel another climax mounting in her core. As Paul lapped and nibbled at her folds, she could feel her tightness heaving with desire for him to thrust his entire dick inside her. Alana couldn't believe this is what she'd been missing out on. With just his tongue, Paul could touch ever center of pleasure in her body. She groaned as his tongue grazed another sensitive part of her pussy.

"Cum for me baby," He demanded again.

Alana cried out as Paul commanded. His tongue was now working feverishly to bring her to orgasm. On his demand, Alana reached another release. She cried out loudly as she came a second time. Again, Paul didn't let up; his tongue continued its assault on her sensitive reddened folds. Alana shuddered and cried out again and again. Her climax seemed never ending. Every inch of her skin was so sensitive to touch that the lightest brush from Paul's tongue sent her crying out in pleasure again.

Finally, he gave her some relief and lifted his head from between her legs.

"Taste yourself baby," He said before kissing Alana on the lips.

Yet again, another act she'd never done. Paul didn't hesitate to press his lips against hers and give her the slightest taste of the sweet juices he'd been lapping up between her legs. The hairs on Alana's forearm stood up as she tasted herself. It was good... Really good.

"Ready for more?" Paul asked.

Alana nodded. She couldn't muster up the energy to say anything more. The orgasms Paul delivered her had almost wiped her out. Still, she felt an urge to feel his hardness between her legs. She was exhausted, but craved more.

Paul got out of bed and stripped down to nothing. Alana ogled his adonis body as he rolled a rubber onto his monstrous member. His dick twitched as he approached her. Alana spread her legs wider and raised them over her head in anticipation of Paul's rough entry.

"Your pussy is so pretty baby," He cooed.

Alana felt wetter with each one of Paul's comments. He didn't just have the magic touch. He had the magic words to ignite her desires in an instant — with a simple statement even. Paul positioned himself between her legs and rested his bulging cock on the outside of her pussy.

43

"Ask for it."

"Ask for it?"

Paul nodded.

"Put it in."

"Not like that…"

"Put your cock inside me…"

"That's better. Now say it with feeling…"

"Put your cock inside me!"

"Beg."

"Please…"

Paul conceded an inch. Alana gasped as she felt his dick stretch her opening ever so slightly.

"Beg!"

"Please… Give me all of it. Shove your big hard cock inside me baby!" Alana cried out.

Paul leaned in close to her and whispered, "Since you asked so nicely…"

In one move he thrust his entire length inside Alana's hot, wet pussy. Even if she'd experienced numerous climaxes, her pussy was still tight and burning with arousal. Once Alana's heat sheathed Paul's hardness, he started to go bad with desire. He began to pummel Alana's tightness with immense force. With each massive thrust, Paul let out a loud groan that reverberated through his bedroom.

To match his bass groans, Alana let out shrill little yelps of pleasure. With each thrust of Paul's powerful cock she felt closer to yet another orgasm. Except this climax would be bigger than all the rest. She'd already been primed for pleasure and she could handle more…

"Harder…" Alana whimpered.

Paul was eager to deliver. He began to thrust into Alana's wetness with even more force. She began to mewl with pleasure as his cock drove into her even more forcefully.

"I'm cumming!" Alana cried out as she announced her big climax.

Hearing that she was close to finish only egged Paul on. He grunted and continued to thrust into her. Alana felt his dick stiffen inside her as she came. She could tell he didn't have long before a climax of her own. Paul took his hand and turned Alana's face towards his as he approached a climax…

Alana looked straight into Paul's cornflower blue eyes with a twisted look of pleasure plastered over her face…

As Paul looked into her eyes he grunted in climax. As he finished, Alana heard him whisper, "I love you Alana…"

When Paul rolled off of her, Alana didn't know what to make of the fact that he'd just told her "I love you". It seemed surreal. She loved Paul too, but she hadn't planned on telling him while he was inside her. Alana was wracking her brain for what to say next when her phone rang.

Alana picked it up and saw the time. *Oh no!*

She was about to be late. *Very* late if she didn't haul her butt out of Paul's apartment.

"Paul, I have to run."

"Already? Is everything alright?"

No. Everything wasn't alright. Alana had completely forgotten the fact that she was about to have a "Psychological Statistics" exam. Her class had been cancelled and she'd cleared up her babysitting schedule last week. Alana couldn't believe she'd forgotten something so important! She had barely studied for said exam due to her night of passion with Paul. Frantic couldn't begin to describe how she was feeling.

"I have my stats exam today and I completely forgot! My professor moved it last week and I didn't even pencil it in!" Alana squealed as she rifled for her clothing amongst the bedsheets.

"Calm down. How much time do you have."

"Thirty minutes…"

"I can drive you there and get you breakfast," Paul offered.

"No," Alana retorted, "Don't worry about it. I'll just take the bus and eat after."

Paul scoffed, "Take the bus? Come on Alana. I'll just put on a shirt and drive you down there."

For some reason, Alana felt more stubborn than usual. She didn't want Paul to bail her out for *her* silly error.

"Just let me run, okay?"

Alana was dressed at that point. She ran over to Paul and kissed him on the lips before fleeing from his house towards the bus stop. Paul might have been right about driving her but Alana felt determined to solve her problem on her own.

The bus stop was a five minute walk from Paul's place… usually. Alana had never walked faster in her life. She made it to the bus stop in two and a half minutes. Once she got there, Alana didn't have to wait long for the bus. Her stomach started broiling in hunger. Alana reached into her tote and couldn't even find her statistics notebook for some last minute studying. She just had to hope and pray that her distraction hadn't cost her an exam grade.

By the time Alana arrived at Warner Hall, she knew that a part of why she had dashed out of Paul's place was the fact that he'd said those three little words to her.

"I love you."

Alana couldn't figure out what scared her so much about those words. She thought that she wanted Paul's love more than anything. Alana guiltily eyed the Cartier bracelet clasped around her wrist. Paul did everything for her. He was sexy, wealthy and he cared about her. Alana just couldn't shake the feeling that their differences were too much for them to overcome.

Maybe it's paranoia...

Alana sat in the exam room and waited for the professor to hand out the exam. She couldn't believe she was thinking about Paul at a time like this. Something about him just took her mind off of everything that was important. Maybe that was the problem — loving Paul meant losing her focus. Just thinking about how much power Paul had over her drove Alana crazy.

She felt like an asshole for running out of his house like that. Alana stared at the blank paper in front of her until she heard the professor ask them to turn over the exam papers and begin. Alana shook any thoughts of Paul from her mind and tried to get her brain into statistic mode.

When Alana saw the first question on the exam, her heart sank. She instantly regretted everything she'd done in the past twenty-four hours *besides* study. Forgetting an exam like this was out of character for her in every possible way. Alana was one of the most organized students in her program and her class rank had been amongst the top ten every year of grad school.

We've got this Alana…

She kept her head down and started writing. Even if she was unprepared, Alana knew she had to at least put forth her best effort. She forced herself to recall formulae she'd thought she'd forgotten and she spent every single moment of the exam working furiously.

When Alana heard the bell ding to indicate the end of the examination she felt shell-shocked. Visions of a C- danced in her head. Alana was sure she'd put her dreams of graduating with a distinction at serious risk. She'd never had such an instantly negative feeling about the outcome of an exam before. Alana couldn't believe she'd allowed herself to do this.

When she left the examination room, her peers were huddled around comparing answers. Alana could feel tears welling in her eyes.

One of her classmates — a competitive Korean man named Thomas — stopped her.

"Alana! Hey Alana! Wait..." He called.

Alana tried to pretend that she didn't hear him but Thomas grabbed her forearm, forcing her to acknowledge him.

"Geez. You look like you've been tortured."

"Yeah..." Alana responded non-committally.

"Well I thought the exam went well. How about you?"

"You know Thomas... I really don't want to talk about the exam right now."

Thomas snickered, "Come on, you aren't fooling me Alana. I know you probably did better than half those gossiping assholes out there. Just... Tell me what you got for number five? I need some peace of mind."

"I promise you Thomas... This was the worst exam of my career."

Thomas tried to hide the grin that was spreading across his face.

"Sorry," He said, noticing Alana's disturbed facial expression, "I can't help but feel like I finally have a chance to unseat you as number three."

Alana rolled her eyes.

"I can't stand you…"

"Listen. We all have bad exams. I'll catch you later, okay?"

"Sure…"

Alana started to walk away.

"Bet you $100 you did better than I did!" Thomas called after her.

Alana didn't feel so confident in her own abilities. She knew that she had a "reputation" for her smarts around her program but Alana still doubted her place here at this university. She had to work for long long isolated hours to maintain her status at the top of the class — it wasn't like she was naturally intelligent or anything. Or was she?

Alana started to walk towards the bus stop. Her heart felt heavy and now that she was alone, she started to feel comfortable shedding a few tears over the whole affair. Her morning had started off so well but after six hours of grueling examinations she couldn't fathom enjoying the rest of the day at all.

She looked at her phone and saw a message from Paul. A lump formed in Alana's throat. If it hadn't been for Paul she would have never been so distracted as to bomb an entire exam. She would have never put her grades at risk by spending the night wrapped up in his arms. Alana boarded the bus and unclasped her new Cartier bracelet, allowing it to rest in her purse.

If she wanted to protect her grades from utter calamity, Alana knew she'd have to end things with Paul. Or at least slow things down. Slow as molasses. Slower, even.

She messaged Paul, "I think we should take a break."

Alana knew it was impulsive but it was the only way she could think of to stop this path of certain destruction. Alana shut off her phone the moment she sent the message. She couldn't bear to see Paul's reply. She knew that he'd try to talk things through. She knew that he'd try to convince her not to slow things down between them.

But Alana didn't want to hear his pleas right now. She just wanted to mourn the outcome of this silly exam and brood over how silly she'd been in the first place. She knew that Paul loved her — but what if his platitudes weren't genuine? When he finally left her, she'd be all alone in the world and she would have given up her chances at real success that was all hers. Paul didn't have to worry about losing a damned thing. He was on the fast track to inheriting a company that had been in the United States since the 1800s.

When the bus stopped in front of Alana's apartment, she made her way up to the second floor and then locked the door. Her apartment looked drab and uncomfortable compared to Paul's house. Alana felt like it was the perfect representation of her life and the differences between them that were constantly threatening to drive them apart.

Paul's home was luxurious, leased by his parents and totally comfortable. He hadn't worked a day in his life for it, but his mother had it fully furnished by an interior decorated who specialized in classic modern design. Alana had worked her butt off to afford this studio on her own. Her furniture had been 90% thrifted. The other 10% she'd managed to buy cheaply from estate sales.

Alana had just promised Paul that she'd leave all this behind to join him in his world up north but from the moment she'd sat in front of that exam paper, she doubted that she'd be able to make good on that promise. How could she eat jumbo shrimp and drink lemonade in Martha's Vineyard when she still had so much to contend with here?

Alana knew she'd done a terrible thing by text messaging Paul her intentions but she always choked when it came to explaining this stuff to him. It was like there was this invisible barrier between them when it came to social class. Alana had no clue how to breach that barrier.

She took a shower, detangled her hair and then plopped down on her shabby chic couch in the living room. Alana had a lump in her throat as she eyed her books on the center table. The next day she had a meeting with her thesis advisor but she couldn't bring herself to actually prepare for the meeting. Alana mustered the energy to make herself a cup of hot tea. Just steeping the fancy loose leaf jasmine in her mug depressed her. Everywhere she looked she saw gifts from Paul... Gifts that made her regret her hasty text message.

BANG. BANG. BANG.

Alana jumped out of her skin.

"ALANA IT'S ME!"

The pounding on her door was followed by a swift
explanation as to who it could possibly be. Paul.
"ALANA! Open up this door!" Paul called to her.

Alana rushed to the door, not because she was
particularly interested in seeing Paul at that moment,
but because she was far less eager in someone filing a
noise complaint against her.

She opened the door to see Paul standing there looking
frantic — but not furious.

"Alana, what the hell?!"

"Come inside Paul," Alana said defeated.

"What the hell is going on Alana?!"

"I'm sorry Paul... I know text message probably
wasn't the best way to do this but I'm serious. Maybe
we should take a break."

"Alana you can't be serious. We just made love for the
first time last night. This morning I told you... I told
you..."

"I know," Alana said. She didn't want Paul to finish. She didn't want to rehash the fact that she'd fled the moment Paul had said the three words she'd been so desperate for him to say before.

"Explain. You owe my an explanation!"

Paul was turning bright red. His pupils were dilated, covering most of the blue in his eyes.

"I bombed my exam Paul! I got so swept up in being with you that I took my mind off of grad school. I can't afford to do this. I can't afford to screw things up!"

Paul grabbed Alana's shoulders and forced her to look him in the eyes.

"Well then tell me to my face that you think our relationship is worth throwing away."
Alana looked into Paul's eyes and all of a sudden felt wrong about telling him she wanted to take a break. The rashness of her text message hit her and she realized what she had almost done. Paul *loved* her. That had to be more important than one test — out of many tests she would get to take.

"Paul… You don't deserve to put up with my crazy okay? Grad school is just getting to me. I can't be as cool as a cucumber like you are!"

"Alana, stop it. You aren't crazy."

Paul placed his finger under Alana's chin. Her lip started quivering as she fought back tears. She couldn't help but feel overemotional about her grades. They were everything she'd worked towards. An achievement oriented woman like Alana couldn't simply "relax".

"I *am*. I am so obsessed with success and I don't know if we're going to make it, okay?"

Paul pulled his arms away and folded them.

"Is that what this is about? You're scared?"

Alana looked down. She hadn't wanted to admit that to Paul.

"Maybe…" She mumbled.

Paul rushed up to her and pressed his lips against hers before Alana could protest. She squeezed her eyes shut and allowed him to kiss her. Tension released in her neck and back as Paul held her close. When he finally released her from his embrace, Alana noticed his sweet blue eyes had softened.

"Don't throw this away Alana. I'm here for you. I'll always be here for you. If you want, I'll help you with your schedule. Just please don't cut and run the moment things get hard Alana," Paul started.

Alana stared at him, unsure of what to say.

"I love you," Paul repeated.

Alana felt the words on the tip of her tongue but something prevented her from saying them. No matter how much Paul reassured her, she was still hard-driving, stubborn and impulsive. He said he could handle her now, but what about after months or years of this. Would he feel so committed then?

"Don't be scared," Paul said, "Just say it Alana. I know you love me too. Just say the words."

"I…"

Alana sighed out loud.

"Fine. I love you Paul."

"Oh come on," Paul teased, a smile plastered across his face.

"I love you!" Alana exclaimed.

"Good," Paul replied, "We'll get through this together okay? I'll help you talk to your professor *if* you failed. I'll make sure that this summer you don't have to worry about a damned thing. Hey maybe you could even get ahead on work."

"Paul," Alana started, unsure if she wanted to get talking about their summer plans.

"Shhh," Paul quieted her down.

"I promise I've got you. Don't throw this all away Alana. I won't let you."

She wrapped her arms around Paul and kissed him on the lips. Alana felt just a little more secure in his arms. Paul soothed her doubts yet again.

---

3 HARD ASS

Alana had been thinking about her insecurities when it came to Paul. She had been suspiciously quick to blame him for her exam troubles and Alana worried that she was using her concerns about school to cover up another issue.

Alana didn't think she had a fear of commitment. But for some reason, she had a hard time truly accepting the idea that Paul might want to be committed to her. She and Paul had hit it off but she couldn't help but worry that Paul would never *really* end up with a woman like her.

It wasn't low self-esteem, it was reality. Men like Paul would inherit millions of dollars someday. On some level that meant Paul's life wasn't his own. His decisions weren't his own. Everything he did had to benefit the Hanover fortune. That was a part of why he was getting an MBA in the first place.

So underneath it all, Alana had her doubts. There was still a chance that Paul would choose being a traditional Hanover over being with her. Alana couldn't imagine that people who'd made their fortune from blood money would be too thrilled with the idea of Paul "sullying" their bloodline.

At least Alana had found out that her panic over the exam had been for naught. As much as she'd panicked about it all, she'd still finished the exam with a B-. It wasn't her usual performance, but it wasn't a failure. Even work had been going well. Alana's latest client — recommended to her by her friend Desiree — paid well. The woman was a bustling thirty-six year old who had a successful online business.

Everything had been going well so there was no excuse for her to feel so… strange about her relationship with Paul. With only a few weeks left until summer, Alana knew she had to tackle this issue at once.

She intended to see Paul that evening at his place. Recently, Alana had been hesitant to invite Paul over to hers. With summer pending, all her focus had gone into her academics and tying up the loose ends with her various odd jobs and babysitting clients. This would be the first summer since she was fourteen that Alana hadn't had to work.

Truth be told, it still made her uncomfortable to feel like she was living off Paul. Even if he said it would all be okay, Alana had her doubts.

She threw on a pair of leggings and a tank top before heading to the bus stop to get to Paul's place. He seemed utterly stress-free about his own upcoming exams. In fact, Alana was sure she'd remembered him mentioning throwing an "exam week bash" for the "business bros". At least he knew better than to invite her to a party that would be held during exam week.

The bus ride over to Paul's was slow; Alana anticipated seeing him even if she was going to bring up a subject she was sure Paul wouldn't want to hear about. When the bus finally pulled up, she started the ten-minute walk to Paul's. Paul's neighborhood was so vastly different from her own. The houses here were more spaced out with huge lawns. Everything was neatly trimmed and well maintained. There was no room for anything that didn't match the Homeowners' Association's pristine view for a Southern neighborhood.

When Alana arrived at Paul's place, she noticed a light on downstairs. She imagined him curled up on his couch with some of his business books and smiled as she pictured a future together where they would live in the same home and share the same space.

Alana rang the doorbell and within moments she came face to face with Paul.

Without saying a word, he wrapped her up in his arms and kissed her on the lips.

"Hello beautiful," He whispered.

Alana hugged him back, inhaling Paul's musky scent and resting her head against his strong powerful chest. Her heart swelled with both love for him and desire at the same time. Ever since their first time together, she'd grown insatiable with desire for more and more intimacy between herself and Paul.

She followed Paul inside, struggling to keep the anxious look off her face. Alana wasn't exactly looking forward to speaking to Paul about serious matters like commitment or their future together.

"How're things?"

"Paul, we need to talk. About something serious," Alana informed him.

Paul — as usual — didn't seem perturbed. Alana wondered how he never seemed anxious about anything.

"Like what?" Paul asked.

Before Alana could butt in, he added, "'Cause I talked to my mom and I have something serious to announce too… We have first class tickets up to Massachusetts! Woo!"

Alana appreciated Paul's enthusiasm but an upgrade to first-class wasn't exactly the level of "serious" she'd been thinking about.

"That's great Paul."

"Let me guess," He said, finally catching on to Alana's mood, "You want to chat about something else?"

Alana nodded.

"You know how the other night I got really freaked out when you said 'I love you'?"

"How could I forget," Paul snorted, "I thought I'd really scared you or something."

"Well," Alana said, "I think a part of that was me being worried about commitment How can I be really sure that you're going to commit to me Paul?"

"Huh?"

"I'm serious Paul! I love you is one thing but what about a future? I have a feeling that your family might not exactly be ecstatic about our relationship."

"My family?" Paul repeated.

He sounded shocked but he mused over Alana's comment for a while. She watched Paul's beautiful blue eyes as he seemed to get lost deep in thought.

After a few minutes of consideration, Paul spoke, "So you want a ring, right? You want me to make this official?"

That was not at all what Alana had intended. Her dark brown eyes widened. It was her turn to ogle Paul with surprise.

"No…" Alana said shakily, "A ring? No Paul, I don't think either of us are ready for that step yet… But I just want… to feel sure, you know?"

Paul pressed his hand to his chin, "Hm… So you don't want a ring but you want to know I'm committed. Can't trust a summer in the Vineyard?"

Alana appreciated his cheeky attempt at a joke but she still needed more from him.

"I want to trust it Paul. I want to trust you... But I'm not a part of your world where it's normal to spend thousands and thousands of dollars on new girlfriends. I want to know that you really value me and I'm not just a pet project."

"You aren't a pet project," Paul reassured her, moving swiftly to hold Alana in his arms.

"Promise?" She asked, looking up into Paul's eyes.

"I promise," Paul replied.

He kissed Alana on the forehead.

"Plus," He continued, "I understand why you're freaked out. But this is truly my pleasure. You work so hard Alana. You work harder than anyone I know. Just let me take care of you for once without sweating it. Okay?"

Alana nodded again.

"I have another idea of how I can show you my commitment anyways," Paul added as an impish look started to cross his face.

"Like what?"

Alana shrieked. Instead of a response, Paul had swept her off her feet. As he hoisted her into the air, he started taking large steps towards his bedroom. Alana wrapped her arms around his neck and giggled as Paul carried her all the way to his bed.

"Any clue what I mean now?" He asked.

"I think I have an idea…"

"Perfect," Paul replied, "But this time Alana… I want to try something new with you."

"Try something new?"

Paul nodded.

"I know we started off taking things nice and slow but I want to ease you into a world of pleasure unlike any you've ever known. But for that to work, I'm going to need you to trust me."

"I already trust you," Alana said, looking deep into Paul's eyes.

She lay back on the bed, propping herself up by her elbows. From this angle, she noticed how tall and powerful Paul looked. He was bulky from weight-lifting and his arms almost ripped through the black t-shirt he was wearing.

"Well I need you to really, really trust me then."

"Paul, what are you saying?"

"I don't want to spoil the fun. How about you just choose a safe word. And if things ever start to head south, you say the safe word and we'll put a stop to to things."

"Okay," Alana said, "Now you're scaring me."

"Don't be scared," Paul said.

The tone in his voice changed. His voice deepened and grew slightly more hypnotic with each word. Alana was entranced.

"Fine then. I'll choose a safe word... How about... How about Peanut Butter."

"Peanut Butter?" Paul said, trying to hold back laughter.

"Yeah. Peanut Butter."

Paul nodded then continued, "Sounds good. Now I just need you to unwind Alana. I've kept all my promises before… And I promise you this time, I will make you see stars…All you have to do is relax. And obey."

When Paul said the word "obey", Alana felt a twitch between her legs.

What was that about? Alana had never considered herself a submissive woman. In every area of her life she'd always dominated. In academics, in her work, in everything. But when it came to the bedroom, Alana found herself pliable to Paul's wishes. She could stand to unwind and let loose, allowing him to take the lead.

"I can obey," Alana replied, toying with the sound of the word on her tongue.

"Good," Paul said sternly, "Now strip down to nothing. I'll be back in a moment…"

Paul left his bedroom and Alana started to strip down until she was butt naked. Her smooth sepia toned skin tingled in the cool air of Paul's bedroom. Alana lay down on her belly, exposing her thick butt and wet pussy to Paul's open door. When he came back he'd have quite the view of his gorgeous, thick girlfriend lying there, eagerly waiting for him.

After a few minutes, Paul returned and when he saw Alana lying there nude as the day she was born he couldn't help but whistle. Alana's physique was undeniably gorgeous. She was curvy in all the right places and she just looked real. Alana's natural, dark skinned beauty stirred Paul's appetite.

"I brought some warm oil," He said, "Stay still…"

Alana remained in her position until Paul found himself on the bed next to her armed with a small bowl of warm oil. Alana gasped as Paul dripped the first few drops of the oil onto her back. The pungent, comforting smell of eucalyptus wafted into Alana's nostrils. As Paul started to rub and massage the oils into her back, she felt a sense of renewal and relaxation fall over her.

He dug his fingers into the knots balled around Alana's shoulders. She groaned loudly as Paul's skillful hands worked out each painful knot. He worked his way down her back until he got to her lower back. Alana could predict that his hands would wander further south…

"Yes…" She whispered inadvertently.

Paul was prepared to give Alana what she wanted and more than what she'd bargained for. His hands began to massage her smooth ass cheeks slowly. Alana moaned again as he massaged each cheek, squeezing them together as he did so. Then his hands wandered down to Alana's thighs. His fingers trailed close to her pussy, wet from desire and lubricated with some of the oil Paul had used to massage her.

"Mmm," Alana groaned.

Paul's finger pushed past her pussy lips and Alana gasped out loud. He held his finger between her pussy lips for a moment and then started to thrust slowly. Alana wriggled her ass to encourage him to plunge his fingers in faster — or even to add more fingers. But Paul just started thrusting his single finger into her pussy slowly.

Alana started panting and Paul rested his thumb outside her puckered asshole and started to massage her forbidden hole.

"Mmm," Alana moaned.

She didn't think that Paul would dare penetrate her most forbidden hole. He kept his finger resting outside her asshole as he continued to probe her pussy. Alana wriggled impatiently, hoping that Paul would give her his hard dick soon...

She gasped. Paul's thumb has pushed past her sphincter and rested just inside her asshole. He removed his index finger from her wetness and added some oil to her ass for more lubrication. Alana squealed as the oil ran down her ass crack and fell into her asshole. Paul's thumb started to plunge in and out of her ass slowly.

Alana had never let another man penetrate her there but Paul was so commanding, so pleasantly in control of the situation that she felt no hesitation allowing him to finger her asshole. He started pushing his thumb deeper and deeper. Alana began to feel unspeakable pleasure mounting inside her. Was this supposed to feel good?

"Ohh," Alana moaned as Paul buried his thumb up to the hilt.

"Sh sh sh," He interrupted her moans, "Don't expend yourself yet…"

Alana gasped as Paul quickly removed his finger from her asshole and stripped down to nothing. Alana maintained her position on the bed. She was just coming to terms with the fact that her boyfriend — perfect, sweet, romantic Paul — was about to put his dick in her ass!

Alana was thrilled by the thought. Its was so naughty, so dirty, so submissive…

She never thought she would be the kind of woman to get up to such things but now that she was in this position — face down with a lubricated asshole, it started to seem like a better and better idea.

Paul eased a condom onto his hardness and hoisted Alana up onto all fours.

"I'll go slow," He promised.

Alana believed him. She had no clue how her body would respond to having Paul's monster dick pounding away at her tight little ass but she had a feeling she'd enjoy every minute of it… If she could handle him at all. She had enjoyed the sensation of Paul's finger moving in and out of her lubricated butt, but feeling his cock would be another story entirely.

Paul slowly pushed his finger into her ass again; Alana arched her back to meet his exploratory digit. When Paul removed his finger from her asshole, he touched the tip of his dick to her tender hole and slowly began to thrust his cock in.

Alana arched her back to allow Paul greater access to her puckered hole. Is this what he meant by commitment? Was he going to give her a mind-blowing experience that changed how she conceptualized pleasure to prove himself? Paul eased his dick in. At first, it hurt badly. Alana winced as Paul's fat dick head squeezed past her tightness.

She wanted to beg for it harder, to feel all the pain of entry all at once. But Alana bit her tongue and allowed Paul to set the pace. He gripped her ass cheeks, spreading them apart as he started to slide his dick in further.

Alana gasped as more of his length started to stretch her out. This *hurt* but it felt good too. Alana didn't understand how pleasure and pain were so closely intermingled. When Paul's full length was embedded deep in her tight ass, the feeling of pain disappeared and she began to feel only pleasure…

Even if Paul's dick was far up her ass, she felt her pussy twitching and convulsing with pleasure. Through her back door he was accessing unheard of pleasure centers and she was starting to experience what she was sure was going to be an earth-shattering orgasm.

Paul started to thrust into her ass.

"Yes! Yes!" Alana cried out.

Paul was starting off nice and slow, allowing her tightness to get used to the invading member. She was already writhing in pleasure and the pain she had experienced had subsided. Alana thrust her hips back to meet Paul's dick. Seeing how much she was enjoying his thrusts, Paul began to plunge into Alana's tight asshole faster and harder.

As his dick slid out of her lubricated heat faster and faster Alana began to emit high pitched moans. She was on the verge of climax and with each thrust she got closer and closer.

"I'm cumming!" She cried out.

Hearing her pleas, Paul grabbed a tuft of her natural hair and pulled her neck back as he thrust into her ass. Alana *loved* this. She loved the feeling like Paul was in control, grabbing onto her and using her ass to pleasure himself. She enjoyed this submissive position so much that she climaxed *hard*. Alana's pussy quivered and convulsed as she came.

Paul was getting close to a climax of his own. Alana could hear him grunting furiously in his position behind her. She groaned and cried out in pleasure, pushing her hips back to meet his cock. Her ass cheeks bounced beautifully around Paul's dick and he found himself unable to hold back even a moment longer.

After a loud groan, Paul released the thickest load of cum he'd ever seen. Alana shuddered as she felt Paul's dick twitch between her ass cheeks. Her tight ass milked his dick of every drop of cum and they were both entirely spent. Paul removed his dick from Alana's asshole and she collapsed onto the bed.

Paul rolled the condom off into the trash then tapped Alana's leg.

"Not so fast missy," He said, "Let's take a shower."

Alana tried to stand up but her legs buckled underneath her. Paul caught her before she hit the ground.

"It was that good huh?"

Alana was still in a daze.

"Mm," She answered.

Paul helped her into the shower and after a few seconds she could stand on her own. Her climax had been so strong that she felt momentarily separated from her body. Paul wasn't joking when he promised that he could give her a world of pleasure unlike any she'd known. Alana wasn't sure if it was the haze of climax talking but she was sure that she could set aside her differences with Paul.

Alana slept over at Paul's that night. In the morning, she had to head to work which meant getting up a bit earlier than Paul needed to. Paul always offered to drop Alana off at work but she preferred to do things on her own. Paul was always trying to help but Alana still grasped at independence where she could — even if she appreciated his offer.

When she woke up in the morning, Paul clung to her before she could get out of bed. Alana tried to wriggle out of his grasp but Paul was tenacious. By the time Alana had eased her way out of his arms, he'd woken himself up.

"Do you really have to leave?" He mumbled.

Alana chuckled, "Yes Paul. I've got to work! You know… That thing you do to get money…"

"Yes, yes, yes…" Paul grumbled.

"Come on, just blow it off."

Alana scoffed, "Easy for you to say."

Paul sat up in bed, revealing his broad chest and mussy hair. Alana suddenly felt that much more tempted to skip work. Of course, she wouldn't. But seeing her sexy boyfriend sitting up in bed was more tempting than she liked to admit.

Paul nodded, "Fine. I'll make you breakfast and maybe you'll change your mind."

Alana was about to stop him but Paul jumped into a pair of boxers and made his way to the kitchen. Alana gestured to him to indicate she was going to take a shower.

Showering at Paul's place always stressed Alana out. He never seemed to have any conditioner and he certainly didn't have cocoa butter lotion or spare wide-tooth combs. Still, Alana tried to do her best to scrub herself down, making a mental note to impress upon Paul the importance of wash cloths.

Once she was done with her shower, she walked towards Paul's kitchen. Alana was immediately hit with the smell of Paul's gourmet breakfast. He'd prepared strips of bacon, fried eggs, rye toast with melted brie, fresh squeezed orange juice and small mugs of espresso. Alana had no clue what sort of magic Paul had pulled together to get this all done so easily.

Alana joined Paul for breakfast. Every single things Paul had prepared was to die for...

"Paul, this is incredible," Alana said.

"Change your mind about heading to work?"

"Paul, you know I can't do that," Alana said, starting to feel frustrated with Paul's persistence.

Alana continued, "I need to work! It's how I keep my bills paid. It's how I'm getting through grad school."

"But you can blow off just one day can't you? You're like a work horse Alana."

"I have to be a work horse."

"Haven't you ever heard the old adage 'D's get degrees'?" Paul said.

Alana just about lost it.

"Paul, just drop it okay!"

Paul's eyes widened. Alana didn't know why he looked so surprised. It was no secret that work was of utmost importance to Alana. She'd repeated over and over again to him why she was the way that she was. Paul couldn't seem to reach over into her world and understand that they came from different places in life.

"Okay...Okay..."

Even if Alana had just asked him to drop the subject, she wasn't ready to. All her frustrations with Paul over his attitude towards her work finally came to a head and Alana snapped.

"I can't just blow everything off because people are relying on me Paul. My mama's relying on me! My family is relying on me! I'm the first person in my family to make it this far and I *need* to make them proud!"

"Come on Alana… Don't you think that's extreme?"

"No! It's not extreme. You just don't get it. You just don't understand what it's like to have family pressure like this!"

Paul scoffed, "Come on Alana… In the next two years I'm going to have to head a multi-million dollar company with *no* experience. You think that's easy?"

"It's not the same thing!" Alana exclaimed.

"Listen, Alana," Paul countered, "It might not be the same thing but it's still a lot of pressure. I'm just trying to tell you that it's not your responsibility to be everyone's savior."

Alana scoffed.

"What?"

"That is just *far* too easy for you to say Paul."

"You don't know how easy or difficult anything is for me Alana," Paul retorted.

Alana could tell she was making him angry but she didn't want to stop. This conflict had been bubbling between them for a while and a part of her just *needed* to lash out at Paul and to get him to lash out at her. Relationships couldn't be all flower petals and roses now, could they? When it came to their differing backgrounds, Alana was tired of pretending it didn't matter.

In moments like this, it clearly did matter and her ability to break through to Paul had been ineffective. Maybe they *needed* to fight for him to finally understand what she was talking about.

"Well Paul, I *need* to help people. I just don't think you get that! I can't just dance the night away every single time you get the whim to do so. People are depending on me!"

Paul shrugged, "Well. I just think you're being a hard ass."

"Excuse me?"

"You don't want to look after yourself and you're blaming other people's reliance on you. But that's not true, isn't it? You just *enjoy* suffering."

"Are you serious right now Paul?!" Alana cried out again, "I don't need to explain myself to you. I have things to do today. I'm just going to leave."

"Some people just need to pull themselves up by their bootstraps Alana. Don't get mad at me for telling you that you deserve to relax!"

Alana stood up and folded her arms, "Their bootstraps? Are you serious?"

Paul leaned back in his chair and calmly replied, "Yes. I'm serious."

"You just don't get me Paul! That's why I've been panicking all this time! I finally understand it. You just don't understand me at all."

"Alana…"

"No! Don't you *dare* say anything sweet. You just get to live your cozy life with Martha's Vineyard and millions of dollars but I've worked all my life since I was fourteen years old! Maybe we just aren't meant to be happy together because I can't lounge by the freaking beach with you when there's work to be done!"

"Alana, you don't mean that."

"I *do* mean that! You just don't get what it's like to be a black woman — the only black woman — in my program. You don't understand what it's like for people to look at you like they're already expecting you to fail. You don't understand what it's like for people to assume that you only got where you are because of affirmative action. You don't get what it's like for people to assume you're some kind of welfare queen looking fro a hand out. You don't get what it's like to live with that pressure every single minute of every single day. You don't get what it's like to feel like you don't belong! You belong everywhere Paul... I don't."

Alana made her way towards the door.

"Alana!"

She whipped her head around and saw from the look on Paul's face that she'd gotten through to him. And she'd upset him.

"Don't leave like this," He pleaded.

"I just want you to think of what it's like to be me for once," Alana begged, "I just want you to realize that maybe I'm not a 'hard ass' because I want to be. Maybe I'm like this because the world never gave me a chance to be anything else. I just want to help the people who got me here."

"I'm sorry Alana."

"It's too late Paul," Alana replied, "The damage is done okay? I want to be sure the man I'm with understands me and... I'm not sure you ever will."

"Jesus Alana, are we back to this again? Are you back to trying to dump me?"

"I don't know."

Paul scoffed, "Well you'd better figure it out."

"Paul... I don't know what you want me to do."

"I want you to just not run away every time there may me problems between us! Jesus Alana. You face so much other bullshit in life but when it comes to you and me... How can I get through to you?"

"Space."

"Space?"

"Just give me some space Paul okay? And time to think."

"We're going to Martha's Vineyard in three weeks Alana. Am I just supposed to ignore you until then?"

Alana sighed. She didn't relish the idea of going without seeing Paul for three weeks but maybe it was for the best. She was growing more and more frustrated with his laissez-faire life and she'd never really considered that the issue might be with her...

"We'll be in touch but I just want a little space, okay Paul? I want to think about us."

Paul stood up and wrapped his arms around Alana, planting a small kiss on her forehead.

"How am I supposed to go three weeks without you?"

Alana looked up into Paul's brilliant blue eyes. She didn't know how she'd go three weeks without him either. But she still felt like she needed the time to get her life in order and prepare for her summer of joining Paul's very new, very different and very white world.

"We'll make it, okay Paul? I just need to work things out on my own."

"Okay."

"And I'm *not* a hard ass okay? I'm just… Under a lot of pressure."

Paul kissed her forehead, "Let's hope you don't crack."

Alana hoped that she wouldn't either. She left Paul's place and still felt uneasy. She'd done just what Paul had warned her against — she'd backed away the moment there was any sign of conflict. She'd impulsively decided on a three week break. Alana realized that perhaps her biggest enemy in this relationship wasn't Paul's ignorance or his whiteness… But herself.

She accused Paul of not understanding her, but she never explained anything about her past. She knew so much about Paul but he didn't know as much about her. He didn't understand that her past was colored by so many things — especially her experiences as a black woman from a poor background.

Alana wondered if Paul would stick around when he found out how she really grew up. She didn't have summer vacations, she didn't have eggs and bacon for breakfast every day. She'd spent many nights hungry, she'd contributed most of her income to her mother as a teenager, she hadn't been able to afford to go to prom.

Alana wondered if her shame was holding her back from Paul. She'd always considered herself a proud, independent black woman. But seeing herself in contrast to Paul brought up emotions that Alana wasn't proud to admit to.

Three weeks. All she had to do was use these three weeks wisely and get out of this bizarre headspace.

I don't want to ruin things with him. He could be the best thing that's every happened to me. Alana thought to herself.

She determined that in Martha's Vineyard, everything would work itself out.

4 MARTHA'S VINEYARD

The first week of the summer was the first time in a *long* time that Alana hadn't had to work. Everything felt strange. Without the buzz of rushing from place to place to place, Alana found a new peace of mind settling over her and a new sense of relaxation in her relationship. She no longer felt worried about school or anything. Alana was close enough to her distinction that she was confident she could get it all done by January when she was fated to graduate. After that she'd be *Doctor Morris* and maybe soon Mrs. Dr. Hanover.

Unfortunately, with the summer change of scenery came a new set of trouble…

Everything had started off alright. Their first class flight to Massachusetts had been beyond comfortable. There were cocktails served throughout the flight and Alana managed to numb the jitters of her flight with two cosmopolitans made with premium liquor. Paul had talked Alana's ear off the entire flight; he seemed excited about finally showing Alana off to his family.

She wasn't sure if Paul was really excited about the prospect of introducing his black girlfriend to his old money family or if he just knew she was nervous and was trying to help her feel better. Either way, Alana appreciated the sentiment. Paul had one younger sister who was fifteen years old and attended Miss Porter's School in New England. She was apparently blonde, a star field hockey player and fluent in French and Italian. They weren't very close but Paul seemed fond of her.

Then he talked about his grandmother, who was the daughter of a British duchess and the American tycoon who brought their family's insurance company into the wealth they had today. Paul's parents sounded both exceedingly proper and exceedingly generous. Paul assured Alana that they would all love her. Then, Paul talked about his cousins. Alana didn't know what to make of his stories. Paul's family seemed to be made up of shrewd business people who had been born into the lap of luxury but still valued good old American hard-work.

Alana still had twinges of unease. Were they really the kind people Paul thought they were, or did they only behave that way when they were around their ilk?

When they touched down in Martha's Vineyard — after transferring from a small plane to a boat — Alana was in awe. She had always heard of wealth like this and she knew that Paul was wealthy. But seeing the kind of wealth he was really surrounded by stunned her. She had never been to a place like this before. Even the small shops seemed practically gilded.

When they arrived at the Hanover Mansion — mansion number two to be precise — that was when Alana's problems started.

She had always suspected that she'd feel out of place in Paul's world but it hadn't sunk in until she arrived there. When Paul's family crowded into the foyer before her, Alana felt like she'd stepped onto a Ralph Lauren runway. She felt too casual, even for just standing in a living room. Paul's younger sister, Cosima, was dressed in a bright floral pastel pink and blue dress. Giant pearls hung around her neck and in her ears. She wore mascara over her blonde lashes and lip gloss on her lips. Paul's mother was dressed almost identically to her.

Both of their blonde strands were pulled back in Burberry headbands and they wore shiny, new looking pairs of Tory Burch flats on their feet. Paul's father was a strapping man who looked like a much older version of his son. Alana was surprised at how old Paul's father look — she guessed that he was seventy or seventy five, meanwhile his wife didn't look a day older than fifty.

Paul's mother spoke first, "Good afternoon, I suppose this is Alana?"

"Yes mother, this is my girlfriend, Alana Morris."

"Pleasure to meet you," Cosima replied, sticking out her hand and giving Alana a death grip handshake.

"Paul," Paul's father grunted, sticking out his hand to do the same.

"And I'm Charlotte," Paul's mother said, giving Alana a limp handshake and a weak smile.

"It's really nice to meet you all," Alana said, "I've heard so much about you."

"What have you heard dear?" Charlotte asked.

Alana mumbled, "Uh... Good things... Mostly."

"PLEASE, Could you speak up dear?"

Alana jumped out of her skin. Paul's nuclear family all took a step to the side and made way for his grandmother who had just emerged from an afternoon nap. Alana didn't know that women that old could even walk, far less unassisted.

"Good afternoon ma'am," Alana said politely, flashing a smile at the old lady.

"Hm," His grandmother replied, ignoring Alana's greeting.

His grandmother eyed Alana up and down and then spoke, "Is she wearing denim in the house?"

Heat rushed to Alana's face. She hadn't known that there was a rule about wearing denim in the house! She looked to Paul (the Third) to see how he responded. He was just grinning from ear to ear while Alana faced humiliation.

"Grandma!" He exclaimed, wrapping the thin old woman in a big hug.

"No need for such excessive sentiments," His grandmother croaked, "Let's get me a smoke, shall we? Then we'll have dinner at once. I want to meet this beautifully colored woman you've brought up here."

Alana flinched when she'd heard colored, unsure if his grandmother's comment was inappropriate or if she had already been made sensitive thanks to the denim comment. Paul pulled away from his grandmother and she looked around from family member to family member.

"Cosima!" She barked.

"Yes grandmother?"

"Do you have any more of those Marlboro's like the ones I found in your desk!"

"Grandmother!" Cosima gasped, turning bright red.

Charlotte looked at her daughter with a pronounced glare.

"What's the big secret?" Paul's grandmother said with a slight smirk across her face.

Alana realized who the person she'd have to contend with in Paul's family would be. Before poor Cosima's humiliation could get any worse, Paul (the Second) handed his mother a cigarette. She started to shuffle towards the balcony flanking the East Wing of the house.

"Why don't I take Alana on a little tour while you have a smoke?"

"And have her change into something less… blue," His grandmother added.

Alana followed Paul as he started to take her on a tour of the house.

"Sorry about my grandmother," He said, "She's old fashioned and quite mischievous."

"I'm so embarrassed Paul!" Alana hissed.

He pulled Alana close and kissed her forehead, "Don't be, alright? I promise you my family will warm up to you. And my grandmother is like that with everyone. Just be chill okay? After tonight, it's just going to be you and me."

After the tour of the house, Alana felt better. Her suite with Paul was luxurious and felt more like a five-star hotel than a part of someone's home. The bed was a cozy king-sized bed and the entire room smelled like lavender. Paul and Alana readied themselves for dinner. Alana ensured not to wear any denim this time. She didn't know if she would be dressed appropriately to meet Paul's picky grandmother but she tried her best. Alana wore a black dress that hugged her curves nicely and fell just below the knee.

Alana didn't bother with any makeup but cinched the new bracelet Paul had gifted to her around her wrist. Maybe with jewelry like this, she'd fit into the entire scene a bit more. Paul didn't seem to understand why Alana was so freaked out by his entire family. A few minutes into meeting them and Alana already felt like she'd botched the entire thing.

Alana tried her best to calm her nerves as they drove to the dinner. She tried to ignore the fact that Paul's grandmother had used the word "colored" to describe her or had talked down about her clothing. They were just *old fashioned.* In no time, they would get used to her.

When they all walked into the swanky restaurant, Alana immediately felt even more out of place. She was the darkest skinned person in the room. She wouldn't have noticed if it weren't for the fact that the wait staff and other patrons clearly did. All of them stared, some of them whispered. She clung to Paul's arm tightly and tried to ignore her discomfort as the stares lingered longer and longer.

"My love," Paul whispered into her ear and kissed her neck before pulling out her chair and seating her down.

Their reservation for dinner was a nice water front table. The waitresses brought out four bottles of Moët to start out for the table. Alana was shocked to see everyone getting a hefty glass of champagne. Even fourteen year old Cosima had a half glass of champagne. Alana noticed that the social boundaries in Paul's world were both rigid and lax at the same time. She had no clue where the boundaries lay or what kind of behavior was expected of her.

Just looking at the menu to order dinner, Alana felt out of place. The cheapest three course option was $200. If it weren't for Paul, she would have never experienced anything like this in her life. She appreciated the luxury but Alana felt anxious too. In a world like this you couldn't afford *not* to be perfect. If this is the world that Paul came from, Alana couldn't understand what it was he saw in her…

Once they'd all ordered dinner, Alana's anxiety picked up. Paul's family was trying to get to know her but Alana still felt like she were facing the Spanish Inquisition.

"So do you golf?" Paul II asked.

"No sir, I don't."

"Please, call me Paul," He said with a smile.

Alana smiled back at him. More because he reminded her of Paul than anything else. Paul II seemed to lose interest in her the moment he realized that she wasn't a golfer.

Then, it was Cosima's turn to inquire about Alana.

"So Paul's your boyfriend right?" She asked.

"Yes, yes he is."

"So you guys have done it right, 'cause I could use some tips."

"COSIMA!" Her mother chastised.

Cosima grinned impishly. It was clear that she had taken after her grandmother and she relished disturbing her family members.

Paul III seemed to find his younger sister funny and he nudged her before saying, "Why don't you wait till you actually have a boyfriend before asking for tips."

"Daddy!" Cosima shrieked.

"Paul. Be good."

Charlotte interrupted, eager to change the subject back to Alana, "So no golf. But what about tennis, dear? You must play tennis."

Alana had taken two weeks of free tennis lessons from the YWCA in her neighborhood but she knew that would hardly count in this world where most people had tennis courts attached to their house.

"No. Not much."

"Not much tennis?" Charlotte said with an air of disdain. It was as if she couldn't even begin to imagine such a world.

"Why don't we chill on the sports talk maybe?" Paul III suggested.

"Good idea, I'm famished," Cosima said, "And I need a smoke."

"You need no such thing young lady," Charlotte hissed.

Her grandmother interjected, "I don't see why she can't have a smoke. In my day, we got started smoking when we were twelve or thirteen."

"You aren't helping," Charlotte hissed.

"Your mother is quite oppressive, Cosima," Paul's grandmother noted.

Before Charlotte could explode, their appetizers were served. For the price of the food, Alana was alarmed at how little food appeared on the table. As everyone dug into their appetizers, Alana hesitated. She picked up her fork and took her first hesitant bite. As she got that first taste of her food, she heard a loud gasp from across the table.

"My heavens!" Paul's grandmother shrieked.

"What is it mother?" Paul II grumbled.

"She's using the wrong fork!" Paul's grandmother hissed.

Charlotte looked over at Alana and shrugged, "Oh honey… Do you not know about all this stuff."

Alana looked over at Paul, hoping he would come to her defense but he seemed totally uninterested in her plight. Alana didn't know about "this stuff" but she had a feeling saying so would draw even more attention to herself…

"I… I need to use the bathroom," She said.

"I think she means the powder room," Paul's grandmother interjected.

Alana pushed her chair back and started walking as briskly as possible to the restaurant's restrooms. Her eyes were filled with tears and she knew that flying up here was a mistake. She'd expected a summer of romance and pleasant interactions with Paul's family. It had barely been six hours and she was already at her limit for discomfort.

They were watching her every motion and judging her as an outsider. Nothing she could do was right and she would always be out of place in Paul's world, just as she predicted. In the bathroom, Alana burst into loud sobs. She couldn't stand to return to that table and face more humiliation but she had no choice. She just wished that Paul would be able to understand.

Alana wiped the tears from her eyes and opened the bathroom door. She knew that she had to pull herself together. Crying never solved everything. What she really needed to do was strengthen her resolve and stop feeling so much shame…

When Alana opened the bathroom door, she saw Paul — her Paul — standing there with his arms folded.

"Alana, are you alright."

She considered lying to him and telling him that everything was okay, but she just couldn't lie to Paul, especially not when she felt like this.

"No, I'm not okay Paul," She said, "I know you think I'm always being some kind of drama queen but I don't fit in here. Your family has made it quite clear that they don't think I fit in here either."

"What do you mean?"

"Are you serious Paul? They're judging me at every turn. I get that I don't have your fancy background... I don't play tennis or squash or golf... I don't have a freaking boat... But I'm still a person!"

"Hey, come here," Paul said, extended his arms to Alana.

"I don't want a hug right now!"

"Come get one anyways."

She reluctantly walked forward and allowed Paul to envelop her in a hug. Alana smelled his cologne and felt safe.

"I want to get out of here Paul."

"Seriously?"

"I'm serious. Say I fell sick and get me a flight down South. I love you… But I can't live like this for ten weeks. It might be normal to you but to me… It sucks. I had such high hopes for the summer and now I don't think I belong here."

"You do belong here," He said, "You belong with me."

"But your family doesn't seem to think so. I'm just the weird "colored" girl who's never going to fit in…"

"Don't say that."

"Paul, listen to me. I'll sit through dinner. I'll play nice… But I need to leave this place, okay? I'm doing this for our relationship."

Paul nodded.

"Whatever you want princess," He said.

His words stung. Alana knew she would be hurting him by leaving but she couldn't see a better solution. She couldn't allow herself to be disrespected like this. Maybe she wouldn't have her all expenses paid summer but at least she was used to hustling. She could never get used to this…

They both survived dinner. Alana couldn't have been more grateful to be free of Paul's family. His grandmother hadn't let up her relentless attack and by the time they'd gotten around to dessert, Alana felt like crying.

Once back in their suite, Alana was determined to book her flight and just get out ofMartha's Vineyard as fast as possible. She couldn't stand staying another day here with the queasy feeling settling in her chest and in the deepest part of her throat. She would much prefer waking up at home in the South. Even if she'd have to work all summer, at least she would be able to put this constant vigilance behind her and just be herself.

Back home, she wouldn't be surrounded by white people who were really judging her for the color of her skin but were too "proper" to come out and say it directly. Instead they picked on the fact that she'd never played tennis or the fact that she wore denim. None of these things seemed to be an issue for Paul; Alana was starting to realize just how different their backgrounds were.

Paul was old money — really, really, really old money. His world was beyond what you'd see in the movies because it didn't have the promise that it was fiction to help you justify and explain away the madness. All of this was real and Alana didn't want any part of it.

"Are you sure you want to leave?" Paul asked.

Alana was absolutely certain. Nothing could change her mind and convince her that staying in Massachusetts to be prodded and harassed would be worth her time. Paul could try, but she was immovable.

"Yes, please. Tomorrow if possible?"

Paul nodded, "So what should I tell my family Alana? They expected you the whole summer?"

"Tell them my mother fell sick."

Paul folded his arms, "Really Alana? You can't just stick it out one more week? You'll get used to them!"

"I don't want to get used to them Paul," Alana replied, "I want to actually feel comfortable."

"Fine, I'll get you my computer and you can book the flights," Paul grumbled.

He pulled his laptop onto the rollout desk in their room and Alana opened it up. She went onto the ticketing website for the boat and then the airline with Paul standing over her shoulder. She could tell that he wanted to say something but she didn't want to turn around and listen to him say it — not right now.

Alana wanted to book her flights first and then handle Paul. He had a special way of being able to talk her down from any and everything. Although she loved him, Alana couldn't allow herself to be harassed by a bunch of snobby people for months on end.

Paul interrupted before she chose her flights.

"Alana, stop," He said.

Alana swiveled her chair around to look at Paul with raised eyebrows.

"I already told you Paul," She started, "Nothing you say will convince me."

"Alana, we've already spoken about your rashness before," He said calmly.

Alana hated how she was already listening to him and how she was already tuned into his voice. His buttery smooth voice reminded her that if she chose to go down South, she'd be losing all this valuable time with Paul. There might be no more difficult family members but there would also be no more Paul — no more kisses, no more cuddles, no more lavish gifts and even more lavish dates.

"I'm not being rash Paul!"

"I think you are."

"So it's not important to you that your family disrespected me like that?"

Paul shrugged, "Of course it's important to me Alana. But we handle things differently you and I. I'm asking you to just listen to my side of things for once."

"Your side?"

Alana was confused. She'd thought Paul understood her and understood why she felt so uncomfortable here. But clearly, he didn't if he thought he could have a "side" in these matters.

"Yes, my side," Paul said, "I know it's frustrating but their antics will die down soon and it will be just you and me. You're giving up the whole summer on a dime! You already knew my family was difficult Alana…"

On some level, it was true. Paul had mentioned his difficult family in the past. But what was just "difficult" for Paul was downright impossible to handle for Alana. She just wasn't used to this. With her black, Southern family, everybody was all jokes and laughter all the time. Aunties and uncles rarely had any problems with each other and all these sly digs and subtle games were non-existent. "Difficult" had a different meaning in Alana's world.

"I'm not saying you've convinced me Paul," She started, worried that he in fact had, "But what if I do stay? What if something like this happens again?"

"I'll do better. I'll stand up for you."

"But the thing is, I'm standing up for myself," She said, "Plus, I'm not sure you'll even realize how much it's bothering me to stand up for me."

"When have I ever broken a promise Alana?" He said, holding onto her hand.

She looked at Paul's hand as it held hers. His pale, large hands were covered in blue veins. The strength in Paul's hands had always been a big turn on to Alana. And now that he was holding onto her tightly, she was softening up to his perspective far more than she expected.

Paul had a strange power over her that no one else seemed to have. Even if her position had been almost transformed, Alana still needed to present her case and ensure that Paul really was hearing her — not just saying what she needed to hear to stay up north with him.

"You've never broken a promise Paul. It's just that I need you to realize how uncomfortable this is for me. I'm the only black person wherever we go and I'm not bougie our anything! I'm just me… Alana. I wear jeans, I've never played tennis and I'm not a part of this fancy fancy world."

Paul pulled Alana up off her seat and brought his lips to her forehead.

"You're a part of my fancy world," He whispered.

Alana closed her eyes and leaned into him, feeling the beating of his heart through his chest and the warmth of his skin. She was already starting to think that staying here was a better idea. At least she'd be able to be close to Paul. Even if she wanted to cut and run, Paul would always be by her side.

"Paul, I don't want to feel like I don't belong here."

He hugged her tightly, "I get it."

"But do you get it Paul? I'm not white. I'll never be white. I'm here and I'm with you but I'm never going to change and fit in perfectly here."

"And that's why I love you," He said.

Alana wrapped her arms around him and kissed him. She'd been hell-bent on leaving New England but of course, Paul managed to prove himself to her again. Sure, Alana had her doubts about his family. But with Paul at least she felt safe. Their different worlds had always been bound to clash. Paul had a good point. If she ran away now, like she always did, their entire relationship would be at risk.

"Our relationship is strong enough to handle this, right?" She asked.

Paul nodded, "Yes…"

He kissed her again. Alana could tell from the way he'd pressed his tongue deep into her mouth that there was far more than kissing on his mind. Her hand eased down to his pants and she could feel his thick member straining through.

"We'll have to be quiet," She whispered.

Paul grinned, "You'll have to be quiet… Not sure you'll be able to though."

"Paul!"

"Don't worry. We have the furthest suite in the house. No one will be able to hear you…"

The mansion was certainly big enough for Alana to believe that claim.

"Strip," Paul whispered into her ear.

Alana felt his warm breath tickling her neck and ears and she couldn't turn him down. She needed Paul almost as badly as he needed her. She eased out of her clothing, standing before him stark naked. Moonlight filtered in through the large, French bedroom windows. Alana's skin was almost tinted blue by the evening light and her supple brown skin shone in the darkness. Paul couldn't wait to wrap his lips around bits of her flesh and then slide in between her sopping wet folds.

Alana's breasts hung in the air, coaxing Paul to nibble on her nipples and take the plump tit flesh into his mouth. He moved in closer to Alana and planted kisses on her neck. As his hot lips touched her neck, chills ran through her body and her pussy grew slick with desire. His lips moved down to her breasts and Alana emitted a soft moan as his mouth wrapped around her hardened nipple.

Paul's tongue grazed back and forth across her nipple until Alana started to grow weak at the knees. Paul swept her off her feet and lay her down on the bed.

"Don't make a sound," He growled.

Alana lay there, naked, spreading her legs to invite Paul between them. At the very least her uncomfortable day could end in mind-blowing pleasure. At the very least that would make it all worth it. Paul stripped down to nothing and then dove between Alana's legs. Before penetrating her, he wanted her to be squirming and moaning, practically begging for his thickness to stretch her folds.

He held her hips down and started to plunge his tongue between her soft, shaven folds. Alana bit down hard on her lip, trying to obey Paul's demand for silence. It was hard… Too hard. His tongue grazed over her engorged clit and surges of pleasure emanated from her core. Alana could feel herself getting wetter and wetter. She bucked her hips to meet Paul's eager tongue. He pressed her hips down into the bed, holding her still.

Heat washed through Alana's body and she got closer and closer to a climax. She knew that she had to be quiet, but Paul's tongue was bringing forth immense pleasure unlike anything she'd ever known. She spread her legs wider and he plunged his tongue deeper. Alana gasped out loud.

"Sh sh sh," Paul said.

Alana bit down on her lip and as she did, Paul slipped two of his fingers between her wet folds. As his hardened fingers slipped into her pussy, Alana came hard. She might not have been able to scream but Paul couldn't stop her quivering and moaning in ecstasy.

"Ready for my cock babe?" He asked.

Alana shuddered and nodded through it all. Paul removed his slippery fingers from between her folds and forced her to taste herself. She suckled on his fingers. Then, Paul stripped to nothing himself and rolled a condom onto his dick.

He positioned himself between her legs and she prepared herself for an entry that would be a lot more difficult to keep quite about. Paul's dick was fully erect and she could tell from the animalistic look in his eyes that he was more than ready to slide into her wet pussy.

Alana grabbed onto Paul's hips as he positioned himself against her. She grabbed his body pulling him closer and he started to slide his hardness inside her. Alana pushed her legs as far back as she could go, allowing him greater access to her wetness. She was close to finishing and Paul could tell.

She threw her head back and her breathing grew labored as her climax approached. Alana clutched at Paul's ass cheeks, forcing him to drive his dick deeper and deeper inside of her. If she was going to stay here she wanted them to make love like this — long and hard and every single day.

"Cum for me baby," He whispered.

Alana exploded. Her juices flowed freely from her pussy and immense heat sprung through ever cell in her body.

"Please, more," She whispered, begging Paul to keep going and to plunge into her harder and faster.

Paul obliged. He pinned her arms above her head, forcing her to remain still in the bed. Alana bit down on her lip to avoid crying out. Her breasts bounced and jiggled with each one of Paul's thrusts. Alana whimpered as another climax surged through her body. His big, hard dick was stretching her out. The Egyptian cotton sheets that covered their large bed rubbed against her back. Alana was surrounded by ecstasy on every level. Paul's scent wafted into her nostrils and each breath brought her closer and closer to another climax.

She wriggled and Paul held her down harder, plunging his cock deeper and deeper into her pussy. Alana groaned, allowing the slightest sound of pleasure to escape her lips in defiance of Paul's command. He was too enveloped in the throes of pleasure to mind her disobedience. Alana could tell he was close to release himself.

Paul released her from his grip and focused on reaching his own climax. Alana watched as his face contorted in pleasure and soon, Paul released inside her. His dick throbbed and twitched as spurts of cum erupted from his staff. He collapsed on top of her. His rock hard abs heaved against her soft, perfectly plump tummy.

Alana wondered if maybe it wasn't such a bad idea to stay on Martha's Vineyard. At least the small island had something to offer besides drama. Paul hopped out of bed and cleaned himself off, returning with a warm rag to assist Alana in cleaning up her juices. She was still unable to move, so spent from the incredible pleasure she'd just experienced.

"Did I convince you to stay?" Paul asked as he crawled back into bed next to her.

Feeling Paul's body next to hers gave Alana renewed inspiration to remain in Martha's Vineyard.

"Of course you did," She whispered, kissing him on the cheek.

Alana hoped that she wasn't making a huge mistake by ignoring her instincts and seceding to Paul's judgment. She was out of her element and ignoring her impulses to just run. Paul had asked her to stay, he'd asked her to change her tendency to escape for them.

I can do it. I can do it for him. Alana convinced herself.

5 THE COUNTRY CLUB

After a few days of life in the big mansion, Alana was starting to see that perhaps she'd made the right choice. Leaving would have compromised her relationship with Paul. He'd been right about his family. After the first night they'd given her that hard time, they mellowed out. His mother, Charlotte, found common ground with Alana in their field of study. Charlotte had done an undergraduates degree in Psychology at the University of Virginia and she seemed very interested in Alana's plans for the future.

Cosima mostly stayed out of the way of everybody; Alana could tell that the spunky teenager didn't have an issue with her and she was far more interested in sneaking off to go boating with her crush or have a cigarette on the back lawn.

Paul's grandmother seemed to have tired out and all she was interested in doing was watching the men play tennis while shouting coaching points at them from the side of the court. With Paul, his father and a few of his cousins available for her to criticize, she had grown quite warm towards Alana.

Alana still didn't feel like she really fit in, but at least things were better and she didn't feel like she had to watch her back. When Paul and his father had to spend time together to discuss business, she was free to walk the compound of the mansion or spend time by the pool reading a good book. Alana had never had so much time to relax in her entire life. She could see why Paul had wanted her here; she could see why he wanted her to rest. Alana felt almost like a hedonist just for enjoying this.

She'd never been more tempted to just give it all up and resign herself to becoming Mrs. Hanover. After a life of struggling, Alana had to force herself to resist.

One morning, Paul informed Alana that they'd be heading over to the country club in the afternoon.

"I'm going to meet up with an old friend of mine, Townsend Wells."

"Huh?" Alana asked.

"Uh, I think you've heard me mention Big-T before?"

Alana tried to hold back a laugh, "Yeah, but his name is Townsend?"

Paul shrugged, "He's the VI of his name. I guess they're attached."

"Your world is just ridiculous," Alana said.

"Yeah?"

Alana nodded, "Oh yeah. Black girls get judged for having names like Lakeisha but I don't know…"

"Well for the record, I think Lakeisha's a beautiful name…"

Alana rolled her eyes, "I'm not talking about you Paul. I mean other white people…"

"Oh."

"I'm just saying. Maybe it goes both ways and we just shouldn't judge each other's names!"

Paul nodded, "You're right. I get it. So… Does this mean you're still coming?"

"Of course!"

"Great. My family's been a member of the club here for over four decades so it will be nice to bring you into the fold."

"Are you sure I'll be welcome in a place like that?" Alana asked.

She knew that Paul wasn't really aware of what life was like for her. He couldn't understand — even if he wanted to — what it was like for her to be a black woman in a place like this that was so separate from her concept of blackness.

"I promise you, you'll be welcome. Plus, I think you'll really like Big-T. He might be a little bit of an asshole, but he'll grow on you."

Alana shrugged, "I'm sure any friend of yours is great."

Paul moved to kiss her on the forehead.

"You're incredible, you know that?"

"Yeah?"

Paul nodded.

"Bringing you up here was the best decision that I ever made. I hope you're enjoying everything despite the shaky start."

"I am..."

"Good. Let's not leave the suite for a bit today, I have other plans for you besides parading you around the island..."

"You do?"

Paul nodded.

"Take your clothes off..."

"Huh?" Alana couldn't tell if he was joking or not.

"I'm serious... Take your clothes off. I have plans for you this morning."

Alana started to shimmy out of the new Lilly Pulitzer dress Charlotte had bought with her until she was standing in a lace bra and lace underwear. Paul ogled her body, biting on his lower lip as he took in all of Alana's beautiful curls.

"Do you remember our safe word?"

Alana nodded, looking up at Paul with bashful eyes. She almost couldn't control it. When she heard him use "that voice", the voice that meant business, she always got into a different head space. In that space in her head, she was prepared to submit to all of Paul's desires. Every craving he could think of, she was prepared to submit to. Alana would do anything to please him; she derived pleasure from pleasing him and submitting completely to whatever he wanted.

"I've been thinking Alana... Now that we're getting closer and closer to each other that it's time for me to start sharing all my desires with you, to start showing you how to meet my needs... Do you understand?"

Alana nodded.

Paul licked his lips, "Yes... I love you very much princess and I also love all the ways you make me feel in bed. But I want us to get more from each other. I want us to tap into all the secret places in our brain where we can feel pleasure and unlock each other's wild side."

Alana nodded again. She remembered when Paul had taken her in the ass and sent her on a wild ride of indescribable pleasure. She remembered how she'd felt afterwards — like she'd become a different person and somehow more bonded to him. That was what Paul wanted more of. He wanted more of her submission. He wanted to use her holes and more. Her wild side had definitely been dormant and vanilla sex had colored all her past relationships.

Paul had exactly what it took to bring her out of her shell and get her nice and comfortable with the side of her that needed to submit.

Paul continued, "So now... I want to do things to you that you've never experienced before okay? I bought a few things that we'll need so I want you to strip down to absolutely nothing, then wait. Use the safe word if you ever want me to stop, alright?"

Alana nodded obediently and then stripped. She lay down on their bed on her stomach, not daring to look back and see what Paul intended to do to her. Paul walked over to the dresser in their room and pulled out some nylon rope as well as an herbal scented lubricant. He pulled Alana's arms behind her back and tied them together tightly, fastening the restraints at her wrist.

Alana tested the binds and realized that she couldn't move her arms. She was essentially trapped lying down on her stomach, at Paul's mercy for whatever he decided to do. She might have expected to feel nervous but all she felt was desire burning within her. She wanted him to take control like this and she was hot with desire for his dick to fill her up.

Paul wasn't satisfied with tying her hands together. He took another set of binds and fastened Alana's legs together too. She was rendered completely immobile. Alana kept silent — there was no need for a safe word yet. Paul propped her up so she was on her knees instead of flat on the bed. Her cheek rested on the sheets and her ass and pussy were both exposed for Paul's pleasures.

He squirted a hefty load of lubricant onto Alana's ass cheeks. Goose flesh prickled across her ass as the cold lubricant started to slide down her voluptuous sepia curves. Paul rubbed the lube all over her beautiful butt and let some ooze into her pussy and butthole. Alana just waited, silently, doing nothing but breathing in and out in anticipation.

Paul was right, this would be unlike anything she'd never experienced. Alana knew then she'd never have to worry about their sex life becoming monotonous and boring. Paul started to rub his fingers along the length of Alana's slit. She twitched as his fingers brushed past her clit with each stroke. She could feel her pussy oozing wetness and she wanted to wriggle away when he stroked her most sensitive parts but she couldn't without falling over.

Paul seemed to enjoy torturing her like this, at least on some level. Alana gasped and moaned and he drove two of his fingers as deep into her pussy as they could go. With his long digits invading her wetness, Alana knew she wouldn't last long. The anticipation alone had brought her alarmingly close to climax. Paul was getting more deliberate with his touch. As he learned the contours of her body, he had gained full control of her pleasure.

Paul removed his fingers from Alana's pussy and she knew where he was going to go next. First, Paul rubbed Alana's puckered asshole with his thumb. Since her ass was just as lubricated as her pussy, Alana predicted his next move. Paul slipped his thumb into her butt and started moving it in and out slowly. This was nearly too much teasing for Alana.

She cried out and almost collapsed on the bed.

Paul removed his fingers from her ass and chuckled, "There there. You haven't even made it to the main event."

She shuddered in anticipation. Paul seemed like he wanted it hard, fast and dirty. Alana knew she'd be shaking and shuddering from his very first thrust. Paul stripped down to nothing and Alana wasn't sure whether or not he'd decided on sheathing his dick. At that point, Alana didn't care. She just wanted to feel Paul's hardness pumping out of any of her holes and pressing her towards an urgent climax.

"Ask me for it Alana," Paul said as he lined his dick up with her asshole.

"Please... Enter me Paul..."

"Ask me to fuck you in the ass."

Alana was hesitant to ask. She could tell from Paul's tone that she was in for a good, hard romp. But did she really want that? Would she really be able to handle it after Paul had already teased her so close to an immense climax.

"Fuck me in the ass," Alana blurted out.

Even if she had her doubts, Alana's instincts pushed her forth and she found herself asking Paul to take her in the ass. Paul didn't allow her a moment to go back on her word. Unless he heard the safe word, he would plunge forth. Alana winced as his dick started to push past her sphincter.

It felt bigger than she remembered and this time, she was unable to brace herself against the bed. All she could do was take it and trust that Paul wouldn't hurt her... At least not badly.

As he started to insert the second half of his cock, Alana grew less worried and she started to focus on the immense amount of pleasure she felt. Paul's teasing had opened her up to pre-orgasmic flurries of pleasure that heralded a far bigger climax once he started to pound into her bottom. Paul's dick stretch her out and Alana let out a loud moan.

"Oh yeah baby… I love it. I love feeling my dick in your tight little ass," Paul growled.

Alana whimpered and he gripped her lubricated ass cheeks as best he could and started to plunge between her eager cheeks. Alana moaned as he thrust deeper and deeper. As he plunged into her satiny heat, she felt his dick delivering pleasure to the deepest, most sensitive zones in her body. Alana knew she was close to a big, big climax.

Paul pounded harder and harder. She came… loudly. Alana cried out, hardly concerned with the possibility that she might be heard.

"Please Paul… Please…" She whimpered.

He continued his hard assault on her ass and Alana continued to moan in pleasure. There was nothing painful about his deep thrusting — all she could feel was almost intolerable physical pleasure and the psychological pleasure that came from the taboo of the experience.

"You like that huh?"

"Yes… Please… More…"

"You like the feeling of my big dick fucking your little ass?"

"Yes! I like it Paul! Fuck me!" She cried out.

Paul had awakened a side in her that she didn't know existed, just as he predicted. Just before Alana was about to reach other climax, Paul removed his dick from her asshole. She shuddered, still afraid to move much out of fear of falling over. She realized then that Paul really had worn protection. He slipped it off and then positioned his throbbing dick at the entrance of her pussy.

It was hot, pumped full with blood and eager to enter her wetness. This time, Alana knew his dick was unsheathed and she couldn't wait to feel his skin rubbing against hers. She was sopping wet and so sensitive she was sure she would cum from the first thrust.

Paul slammed his cock into her pussy in one swift motion and Alana cried out loudly. She could imagine the impish grin on Paul's face as he watched her beneath him, tied up so tightly she couldn't move, writhing in pleasure. Paul gripped her ass cheeks and pumped into her hard and fast. Alana cried out again in a quick climax. Her legs shuddered and she almost collapsed again.

Paul repositioned her and continued his manic thrusts. He was close to his own finish, Alana could tell. She moaned and swiveled her hips as much as she could to egg him on. Paul started to thrust slower and slower, then finally he emitted an animalistic grunt and removed his dick in a swift motion. Paul grunted again and Alana felt his hot seed spurting onto her ass cheeks.

She was shuddering with pleasure and they were both short of breath from their intense, hard romp. They just held their positions for a few moments, catching their breath and trying to process the intense pleasure that had just jolted through both of their bodies.

Once the intensity had died down, Paul slowly made his way towards Alana and unfastened her binds. Her wrists showed deep indentations where the ropes had bound her but at least Alana could be assured that they wouldn't turn bright red. Paul helped clean her up with a warm rag and then suggested with an impish grin, "Shower?"

How could Alana resist taking a shower with him? After an experience like that, she felt incredibly bonded to Paul. In submitting to him, he'd never once betrayed her trust. Her submission didn't mean relinquishing power — in fact, Alana had never felt more powerful during love-making. Whatever it was Paul had awakened in her, Alana liked it.

She didn't know what her afternoon would bring, but she was starting to think that coming to Martha's Vineyard wasn't such a bad idea. She'd become more liberated in so many ways, especially sexually. Things were good with Paul. And they were getting better.

Alana still worried about this bizarre world she had entered, but given everything that was going on in the bedroom, she was willing to stick it out unless something truly egregious happened.

In the afternoon, they were headed to the country club. The theme of dress was "all-white" which of course, added to Alana's anxiety. She couldn't help but have a feeling that dress code wasn't just about what you were wearing. Of course, Paul was totally ignorant to her plight. Alana didn't usually wear all white so she had to borrow something from Paul's mother. Charlotte had offered Alana one of fifteen dresses to select from and Alana was having a hard time choosing.

"Paul, I have no clue what to wear, do you think this is too formal?" She asked, spinning around in front of the mirror.

Paul shrugged.

"No clue babe, I think it looks fantastic."

Alana's frustration with him was mounting. After their incredible romp that morning, it was amazing how quickly Paul could start getting on her nerves. She didn't just want him to tell her that she looked fantastic. She wanted to actually fit in.

"I'm not asking if you if it looks fantastic Paul. I'm trying to fit in…"

"Just be yourself," He said, planting a kiss on her cheek.

As much as Alana wanted him to get it, sometimes Paul could be just clueless. This was something she'd been struggling with on and off. Every time Paul reassured her, he bounced back with some other comment or passive disinterest that let Alana know he was clueless.

Being color blind might work for their relationship but it was impossible for Alana to really navigate the world as "color blind". She didn't choose to be judged for the color of her skin, she just was.

Without Paul's help, she settled on a slim fitting white halter dress that cinched tightly around her waist. Charlotte was a little bit slimmer than Alana and she certainly didn't have Alana's round buttocks and full bosom.

When they drove past the country club security, Alana was a bundle of nerves. She tried to hide it from Paul as best as she could. He was calm, comfortable. She tried to imitate his demeanor and keep her mind off of her fear. She wasn't sure how she would like Paul's friend 'Big-T' either. Paul tended to have good judgment in people but Alana was still just… nervous.

Paul helped her out of the car and linked arms with her as they walked into the entrance. When they entered the country club, Alana realized that her suspicions had been right. Nearly all the wait staff stared at her immediately. Their eyes bore holes in her lily white dress. Alana imagined for a moment that they were lasers, exposing her dark skin beneath the dress to greater scrutiny.

"Welcome," A smiling waitress said, her eyes glued on Alana even if she was speaking to Paul.

"Hello ma'am. I'm Paul Hanover. I have a reservation with Mr. Wells."

"Oh yes, the rest of your party is over there. I'll take you to his table. Is your friend coming with you?" The waitress asked.

Alana cringed, suddenly feeling small. She knew the waitress had done it on purpose. Her arms were linked with Paul's and it was clear to anyone that they were definitely not there as "friends". The slight act of aggression might not hold up in a courtroom, but Alana was accustomed to that squeamish feeling of covert racism that she'd felt many times before throughout her career in academia.

"My girlfriend will be joining me, yes."

Again, Paul didn't seem to notice. Even if he'd corrected the waitress, he seemed nonplussed. Alana held onto him tightly and they weaved through the tables and chairs to the back corner where Townsend Wells was seated. As they walked through the tables, every pair of eyes was glued on Alana. She wanted to shrivel up and go unnoticed but they denied her the decency of anonymity. Their cold eyes wanted to know why an outsider was in their space — especially an outsider that was the "wrong" color.

They joined Townsend's table and Paul introduced Alana enthusiastically. The eyes hadn't stopped staring at her and Alana could even pick up on a few whispers that she tried to tune out.

"So this is the famous Alana," Townsend asked, "How do you like the Vineyard?"

Alana found Townsend friendly and warm enough. He was far less handsome than Paul in almost every way. He was pale, with short coarse blond hair and big buck teeth. His eyes were a brilliant shade of blue and his nose erupted from his face like it didn't belong there. Townsend was almost terrifyingly thin too.

"It's really lovely up here. Different from the South."

Townsend nodded, "I see what you mean. The North is far less racist than the South anyways. We have… class up here. Know what I mean?"

"Hey, watch yourself," Paul teased.

The two men laughed. Alana didn't know what to make of it. If the North was less racist than the South, why did she feel more out of place here than she'd ever felt in Atlanta.

"So how are you doing buddy?"

Before Townsend answered, they all ordered drinks. Alana had a feeling she'd need one. The men ordered nice cognac on ice and Alana ordered a large margarita.

"I'm doing great. Recently my brother, Jack, won his seat in Congress."

"Where's he based out of again?"

"Pennsylvania. Terrible state."

"Right, and what about Teddy? I haven't seen that guy in a long time."

Alana hoped she'd get a chance to zone out and ignore the rest of their conversation. She wasn't interested in what all these people — people she didn't know — were up to. Her insights into Paul's world had been both good and bad. She loved the nice restaurants, the shopping and the delicious food. She couldn't stand the boring conversations about politics and old prep school buddies.

"Teddy?" Big-T repeated, "Well I think he's involved in the gubernatorial race over in Wyoming. He's finally given up on skiing and picking up slope sluts."

He continued, "Did I ever mention to you that I and my father are involved in funding the Massachusetts gubernatorial race ourselves? It's a tad more important than Wyoming…"

"Really?" Paul asked, taking a large gulp of his gin drink, "Is it any of the Eaglebrook boys who're still kicking around here?"

Townsend smiled, "Good guess. We're getting Buck to try to run this year. Remember Buck Baskin?"

"He graduated a few years before we did, correct?"

Paul nodded.

"Governor Baskin will be honestly perfect for the job. He's got a good handle on the nigger problem in Boston and he'll lower taxes for those of us who're pinching our pennies."

Alana's eyes widened at Townsend's causal usage of the n-word. He'd said it so freely as if he used it often, and he didn't flinch or make eye contact with Alana or seem to feel any sort of shame. This was the type of incident that thrust Alana into a whirlwind of emotions where she didn't know what to do or what to say for a moment.

This was the sort of thing where everyone looking from the outside would *think* that they knew how to react.

"I would have punched him in the face," They might say. Or something.

Alana just sat with her mouth agape trying to figure out *what* to say. She knew she had to say something but she was also in a precarious position. She was already an outsider in this country club; if she started a fight, she would be the angry black woman and the aggressor. If she even spoke up, she had no idea what she'd face.

But Alana knew she had to say something.

"I'm sorry, what did you just say?" She interrupted.

Paul looked at her confused, as did Townsend.

"Just talking about our buddy Buck. He'll handle the nigger problem in Boston really well."

Again, Townsend didn't flinch and his face betrayed none of his emotions. Alana couldn't tell if he was taunting her or genuinely ignorant.

"Yeah," She said, trying to steady the shaking in her voice, "That's the problem... That's a slur."

Townsend laughed — a big hearty laugh that came up from his belly and reverberated across the room.

"Listen cupcake, there's a difference between black people and niggers right? It's not racist, it's just a way of differentiating."

He then returned to talking to Paul as if his analysis had settled the matter and there was nothing more to discuss. The conversation shifted quickly and Alana couldn't get a word in without seeming like she was fixating on the issue. But *of course* she was fixating. Townsend had just used the n-word casually in conversation like it was "milk" or "the". What made it all worse was that Paul had said nothing; he hadn't even backed her up.

Alana sat back and finished her drink, motioning to the waitress for another one. If she was supposed to sit here with Paul afternoon she wanted to be sufficiently drunk. This was proof that what she'd been worried about had been correct all along. Paul's world didn't align with hers. Where Alana came from, she'd never met a white person who'd dared to call her the n-word — aside from maybe drive by motorcyclists.

Now she was trapped in this strange place where if she spoke out, her words would be twisted and the meaning of things could be confused.

If there was a difference between "niggers" and black people as Townsend said, what did that make her? And how far away was she from becoming one of those he deemed unworthy? Alana wasn't wealthy, she had two uncles who had been in prison for years, one of her second cousins was a recovering addict. And though her family had problems, they were all loving people who had each other's back no matter what. The way people in this world stereotyped and judged was driving Alana mad.

She seethed as she pounded back another drink. With two drinks in her system, Alana thought she would feel relaxed but really that was all she could do to prevent anger from bubbling to the surface and exploding in a dramatic way.

This was what she had always feared; Paul's apathy towards her distress in situations like this would tear them apart. Now, Alana couldn't figure out how much pleasure, how much love would be worth feeling so degraded and worthless.

She survived the encounter but as they walked out of the country club together, her eyes were glazed over. She tried to fight back the tears she'd done a good job of holding back inside the country club. Paul continued to talk her ear off about how nice it was that he'd gotten to see Big-T again and how they should go out for drinks in a few days. At this point, Alana's throat was so tight that she couldn't reply.

"Hey are you alright?" Paul asked once they were in his car.

"No."

Alana knew if she wasn't short, she'd risk exploding.

"Didn't like Big-T much? He can take some getting used to…"

Paul's naïve ignorance pushed her over the edge.

"Take some getting used to? Paul, are you out of your mind? This guy used the n-word in front of me without even flinching?! Are you telling me that you just didn't notice that? Are you telling me that's fine?!"

Paul looked baffled at Alana's explosion. She wouldn't let him get into her head and make excuses or justify this. She had every reason to feel upset. Racial slurs were never "just words" and Alana wasn't simply "offended" — she was shocked, she was disgusted, she was reminded of the fact that no matter how hard she worked and how much she accomplished some people would always see her as sub-human.

"I didn't think you'd react that way."

Alana shouldn't have been surprised by Paul's casual response. He *never* seemed to think about these things which was exactly the issue. He was flawless in every other way but there was some part of him that just couldn't see Alana's perspective; he was far too insulated from her reality whereas she had to adapt and shift to his…

"You didn't think I'd react that way? You think that I'd just be fine with someone using the n-word? Do you even know me Paul?" Alana snapped.

"I'm sorry."

"Sorry just isn't enough Paul!" Alana replied, "I'm hurting and you don't notice. You don't notice racism. I mean, do you think that I get the privilege of just ignoring everything that happens when it comes to race? Because I don't."

"Well what do you want me to do Alana?"

"I want you to just show that you care Paul! I want a man who understands what I go through on a daily basis. I want a man who stands up for me!"

Alana couldn't hold back her tears at this point. She'd held back her emotions throughout their entire meet up with Townsend and now she was realizing just how hurt she was. She *wanted* Paul to swoop in and defend her. It was just instinct — she wanted to feel like the man by her side could protect her from all the ills of the world.

They arrived at the Hanover mansion and Alana got out of the car, marching to the suite with Paul chasing behind her. She just needed to be alone instead of listening to Paul's platitudes.

"Wait, Alana!" He called after her.

She didn't stop moving until Paul finally caught onto her arm.

"Alana, please, don't do this. I'll find a way to make it better. I'm sorry this keeps happening."

"Do you think it will ever stop happening Paul?" She asked, turning to him with tears still streaming down her face.

She looked at her perfect boyfriend, tall and handsome with his cornflower blue eyes. She searched those beautiful eyes for some sort of reassurance that maybe, maybe this was what would change his mind. Maybe he would finally realize that change needed to happen.

"I can't just be the pretty, quiet wife on your arm," She continued, "I can't be that person and if that's the person you need, if that's the person you want, we'll have to go our separate ways Paul. I don't want it to come to this."

Paul nodded, "I understand."

Alana hoped he would say more, but of course he didn't. She had no clue what to make of Paul's silence and what it meant for the future of their relationship. The argument felt staunchly unresolved and Alana had no clue how the next few weeks would play out.

6 I'LL BE SEEING YOU

Their night together was disturbingly quiet. Alana didn't think that she had anything else to say to Paul. But Paul's silence was what unnerved her. Paul was never quiet. He was the life of the party, the man about the town, the great initiator of any and all things fun and exciting in his world. He wasn't the kind of man who could quiet down about anything. Alana wondered if her words had really resonated with him. Maybe he was thinking this through. Maybe this would be the catalyst for change.

In the evening after dinner time, Alana was starting to worry. Paul's noted silence was starting to make her think that something was wrong. She knew that she'd been in the right so whatever Paul was struggling with had to be internal.

Eventually, he made his way over to Alana where she was reading on the chair.

"Alana," He said, "Can we talk?"

Alana felt a lump in her throat. She had no qualms about talking to Paul usually, especially not about difficult things, but she could tell from the look on his face that this wouldn't be one of those conversations that ended in something positive.

"Sure."

Paul sat down across from Alana and buried his head in his hands.

"I've been thinking for a while Alana and what I think is we need to stop seeing each other."

Alana looked at him in surprise. Paul had begged her not to do anything impulsive and end their relationship. He'd begged her to come all the way to Martha's Vineyard and leave behind a summer of earnings. She loved him. She'd sacrificed everything comfortable for him and now he was suggesting throwing it all away…

"Paul, are you serious?"

Paul nodded grimly.

"I've put you through a lot Alana and I can't stand to put you through any more pain. I know I have a lot of work to do but that doesn't mean you have to suffer while I do it."

"Paul, I'm not suffering!"

"Yes, yes you are Alana. I can see your hurt even if you try to hide it from me."

"But if you break up with me, how am I going to get back to Atlanta?!"

Alana was getting frantic. She couldn't emotionally process what was happening. She wanted to beg Paul not to do this but she could tell that he couldn't be convinced otherwise. Paul was the type of man who was immovable once he'd decided upon something. While he could always change her mind, Alana had never had the same power over Paul.

Paul nodded at her question, "Listen, I have it all worked out Alana. I'll book the next flight out of here tomorrow and I'll transfer $20,000 to your account to make up for the trouble I've put you through this summer. You still won't have to work or anything."

"Paul, I can't accept $20,000 from you."

"You can," He continued, "You know that I can afford to do this Alana so just let's end this alright? We'll have a clean break and you can start your life over once the final semester picks up."

Alana realized that he was serious. He'd figured out how all of this mess could be worked out and realizing that he could do this without ruining Alana's life, he planned to go through with it.

"But what about your family Paul?" Alana said, her lip quivering as she realized that by saying this she was acknowledging Paul's break-up. She was acquiescing to the fact that their relationship would be over.

"I'll tell them the truth eventually."

"I don't want to leave you Paul…"

"I don't want to leave you either, Alana," He said, "But I'd rather leave you than keep hurting you over and over again."

Alana stood up and Paul joined her, moving close to her and wrapping her in a hug. Alana just stood there, allowing him to hug her as tears began to flow freely down her face. Alana looked up at Paul and got on her tip toes to kiss him. He kissed her back…

"What about everything we talked about Paul?" Alana whispered through her tears.

Paul shrugged, "I don't know…"

"We were supposed to have kids, have a family together. That's really all over?"

Paul nodded, "It has to be Alana... And I promise you, if we're meant to be together we'll find our way back..."

Alana kissed him again. She was angry, sad, upset and at the very least, she wanted to be with Paul one last time. She grabbed below the belt and Paul pulled away.

"Alana... Stop..."

"I want you Paul," She whispered as she stood there with tears in her eyes. Even while crying she looked absolutely beautiful.

Paul cautioned, "If this happens Alana, this is the last time. This is really it."

Alana nodded. She understood Paul's perspective. While she couldn't believe that he was really ending things between them, she understood and she respected his choice. She'd collect her money and she'd be on the next plane to Atlanta and then the healing would have to begin. For now, she didn't necessarily want healing. She just wanted to feel something. She just wanted to touch Paul one last time...

"This is it," She whispered.

Alana was having a hard time accepting it. At least she'd have this fond memory as closure to look back on…

She undid Paul's belt buckle and pulled his pants and underwear to the ground. His dick was already rock hard. It didn't take much for Alana to arouse him. She dropped to her knees before Paul and grasped his large, hardened member in her hands. As her small soft hands gripped his cock she started to pump at the base to lengthen him further.

Then, Alana stuck her tongue out and flicked it across the head of Paul's dick. He shuddered. Alana felt powerless to stop Paul from ending their relationship, but she at least had the power to give him pleasure that no one else could. She had the power to bring him to climax after climax in a way that no one else could compare to.

She took his bulging dick head into her mouth and started to suck on the sensitive, engorged head. Alana felt Paul's dick throbbing fantastically in her mouth as she focused her attention on only his head, teasing him as she purposefully avoided the shaft.

Alana decided that it was time to end the teasing and she took all of Paul's large shaft down her throat. Paul groaned as she engulfed his entire member in her hot, wet mouth. Alana started to move her mouth up and down his entire length. More saliva surrounded his dick and the blowjob started to get very wet, very fast. She knew after arousing Paul this much, he wouldn't stand for just a blowjob and he'd want to ensure that he at least got to make love to Alana one last time.

She took him deeper and deeper into her mouth until as she predicted, Paul stopped her and removed her from her position on his cock.

"Take everything off Alana," He said.

Paul was still his dominant self but Alana could detect the slightest hint of sadness in his voice. He didn't want to break up with her but for some reason, he felt like he had to. Alana wished that he didn't feel like that. She wished that this encounter wasn't so heavily colored by the harsh sadness of goodbye.

She obeyed, slowly slipping her clothing off her shoulders until she just stood in her underwear. Paul's eyes remained glued to her so she removed her bra, allowing her full bosom to swing into view. When Alana slipped off her underwear, Paul ogled her freshly shaven pussy.

Would he miss this as much as she would? Would he move on quickly? Alana didn't want this to be over. As she stood naked before Paul and realized this was the last time she'd ever be doing this, her heart was shattered.

"Kiss me," She asked, worried if she did or said anything else she would burst into tears again.

Paul conceded to her request and he kissed her lips over and over again. Then his lips wandered to her neck and Alana closed her eyes, taking in every moment, forging the memory as best she could. She inhaled Paul's glorious musk and the scent of his shampoo lingering in his hair.

As Paul's hands traveled down her hips and lingered outside her pussy lips. Alana gasped as Paul's index finger pushed past her entrance and he began to probe around her wetness. He stroked the sensitive inner walls of her pussy until she was having trouble standing up. Alana gasped as Paul started to graze his fingers across the most sensitive parts of her wetness.

"Paul... Paul..." Alana whimpered.

Paul removed his fingers from her wetness and carried Alana onto the bed. He lay her on her back and pushed her legs into the air so her wet pussy was spread open to him. Paul positioned himself between Alana's legs and ran his fingers along the length of her pussy.

Alana quivered in anticipation and desire. Paul bent his head between Alana's legs. She gripped the bed sheets as Paul's tongue made its first contact with her wetness. Alana cried out as He fastened his lips around her engorged nub. Paul suckled on the little nub of pleasure and then rubbed his tongue over it back and forth faster and faster.

Alana's breathing became labored and as she gasped for breath, she felt a quick climax mounting in her body. Her skin grew hot and her heart raced. She let out a loud cry as she exploded in pleasure again. Paul pushed his tongue deeper between her folds then rubbed his tongue against her very wet folds.

She spread her legs wider allowing Paul greater access to her pleasure center between her legs. He flattened his tongue and continued to slurp at her wetness with broad strokes. Alana climaxed again. This time, juices gushed out of her pussy and she convulsed in absolute pleasure.

Paul removed his face from Alana's pussy and pressed his lips to hers. Paul allowed her to taste herself and drove his tongue into her mouth, amping up Alana's desire for him. Alana gripped Paul's body, holding him close, encouraging him to kiss her more and more. If this was really going to be the last time, she wanted it to be worth it. She wanted to ooze all the love she could out of every kiss, every touch, every beautiful moment that their skin touched.

Alana could have suspended this moment in time forever just so she could keep Paul here, just so she could stay in Massachusetts with him instead of starting over when she least expected it.

Paul moved off of her and hastily removed his shirt. Alana felt her pussy grow slick again at the sight of Paul's rock hard abs. He moved between her legs swiftly and shoved his hardness into her all at once. Alana gasped as she felt Paul's massive member invading her tight hole. Even if she was slick, her pussy still ached as she attempted to accommodate Paul's sizable cock.

"Fuck me," Alana whimpered.

Paul started to move his hips, thrusting his dick into her nice and slow. With each teasing stroke, he moved Alana closer to a massive climax. She grabbed onto Paul's back and felt his muscles pulsing beneath her finger tips with each stroke. Alana looked into Paul's eyes. As they made eye contact he picked up the pace and started to enter her more furiously. Each stroke was packed with emotion. Alana felt his skin beneath her finger tips and with the heat of his passion, she grew closer still to climax.

Paul bent his head to Alana's and pressed his lips to hers. Feeling his lips on hers and his cock buried in her wetness, Alana couldn't resist a big climax. She shuddered as she released deep inside of Paul.

"Yes… Yes Paul…" Alana moaned breathily.

Her pussy contracted around his cock, gripping it like a vice and pushing him towards a release of his own. Paul started to pound into Alana harder and harder. She groaned in ecstasy as she felt his cock starting to ram in and out of her wetness. She dug her nails into Paul's back and his silence transformed into animalistic grunts of pleasure.

Alana continued to shudder and moan, "Yes Paul… Give it to me… Yes…"

Alana egged him on and wrapped her legs around Paul tightly. She felt his ass moving rhythmically as he continued to bury his dick deep inside her pussy. Alana climaxed again and this time she could feel Paul was getting close.

She threw her legs behind her head again and moaned until she felt Paul shudder. He removed his dick from her pussy as quickly as possible and let out a loud groan of pleasure as he erupted onto Alana's tummy. His dick twitched three or four times and a giant load landed on Alana's belly. Her tummy heaved up and down as Paul's spilled seed lay there in a glorious mess.

Paul was still a gentleman, even if things were over between them. He cleaned Alana up with a warm rag. She couldn't bear to remain undressed next to him. Even if they'd just made love, to Alana this was final. Her heart had been ripped out of her chest and doing anything to confuse where she stood with Paul would only make the gnawing worse in weeks to come. Alana knew that much.

They'd connected so well in bed that it was almost easy to forget how incongruent their cultures were in the outside world.

But after they'd made love, as promised, Paul booked Alana the next boat off the island and the next flight back down to Atlanta. Then Alana watched him wire $20,000 to her bank account. After he did, she collapsed in tears. That final act solidified in her mind the notion that she was no longer Paul's girl. She wouldn't be Mrs. Hanover. She would be Dr. Alana Morris come January, but she wouldn't have a future to look forward to with Paul.

This beautiful, beautiful thing was now over. And Alana couldn't see a world in which she could get Paul back. He was convinced that he'd caused too much trouble for her and Alana couldn't exactly lie and say that she hadn't. Their differences had pushed them apart and there was nothing she could do except accept what had likely been inevitable.

Alana flew back to Atlanta the next day. The entire flight, she stared morosely out the window, wishing that she could be as carefree as the clouds in the sky. She missed him. She missed Paul. And she had no clue how she was going to readjust to what life would be like without him. Paul had meant the world to her. While she was troubled by their differences she never thought they would actually mean the downfall of their relationship, especially since she had traveled so far for him and given up so much.

The last weeks of the summer passed. Alana lived as frugally as possible on her $20,000 and still picked up as many babysitting gigs as she could. Her friend Desiree was willing to help her find rich mothers who needed help and Alana found herself nannying for a few NFL wives and basketball wives in the city. She was making good money as a nanny and preparing for her final semester.

Alana's pending success didn't feel as good as she thought it would feel. She had figured that even without Paul, she could still celebrate the fact that she was about to be Dr. Morris. She would be able to work as an apprentice therapist for a few years and then start raking in the cash. Alana knew she was in a good place in terms of her career, but it just didn't feel good. Alana's anhedonia extended to other aspects of her life.

She had little to no interest in dating anyone else. She could only think of Paul. For the end of the summer, Alana had tried not to stay in touch with him. Paul would send her messages and tell her that he was thinking of her but Alana could hardly bear to respond. If Paul wasn't by her side, what was the point in keeping up any sort of relationship between them? All it would do would be to hurt her... Badly.

Alana's apartment lost its shiny luster too. She had no desire to be as neat as she used to be and she found it much easier to get swept up into chaos. She'd changed into a person that she hardly recognized. While externally, few people could detect a difference, Alana felt different on the inside.

Losing Paul had been like having surgery without anesthesia. The wounds ached long after they should have healed. When the semester started up again, Alana was convinced that she'd never be okay. The chances of running into Paul again had increased ten-fold and Alana found herself anxiously gazing over her shoulder and avoiding areas of the city and campus where she knew that she might see him.

Alana's hair had grown down to her waist but her morning ritual no longer involved such meticulous care towards her appearance. She still got her nails done every once in a while but she mostly piled her natural hair in a big messy bun on the top of her head. She found herself wearing leggings and a sweatshirt a lot more than she wore a nice button down and a pencil skirt.

After a morning meeting with her mentor during the first week of school, Alana realized that she'd have to go to the registrar's office to work out the details of her graduation plans. Everyone in her family wanted to be there and Alana realized she might have to sweet talk a few administrators to get over twenty tickets for her graduation ceremony.

Alana made her way to the registrar's. The South was still nice and warm; Alana didn't look forward to Atlanta growing colder and colder. Alana already needed to wear a nice sweater. As she left her house, she clasped the Cartier bracelet that Paul had given to her around her wrist. Alana had considered selling the bracelet or at least tucking it away. But she couldn't help but wear the beautiful set of jewels around her wrist.

The registrar's office luckily wasn't very crowded. Alana made her way to the front of the office and started waiting in the short line. She looked around, terrified that she'd run into Paul again. This was one of the places on campus where their lives were likely to intersect. It had been almost three months since they'd parted ways in New England and Alana didn't want him to get even a glimpse of an idea of how much of a wreck she was.

Alana was sure he would have moved on already. She replayed the day that they'd broken up in her head over and over again. There had hardly been a fight. He had just been tired of hurting her. That made the breakup cut her even deeper. They both still loved each other deeply. Alana still hadn't let go of the idea of the future they had promised each other. She had pictured a beautiful wedding and beautiful children. Seeing him again would just remind her that none of that would be possible.

She popped in her headphones. There were two people left in line ahead of her. As Alana sat there, a man joined her on the bench.
"Alana, hi!"

She looked to her right. The guy who had joined her was a white guy who had taken a few psychology courses with her in her first year of graduate school. He was tall, handsome and played lacrosse too. Alana couldn't quite recall his first name though...

"Not sure if you remember me from our seminar the first year. It's Brent."

Right. Brent. He'd been cute and flirty in their classes together but he'd never really pursued Alana. In fact, Alana was almost certain that at the time, she'd discovered that Brent had a girlfriend.

"No, of course I remember you!"

"What are you up to here, getting grad school invites?"

"Yeah, I'm trying to convince them to let my big crazy family onto campus."

Brent grinned, "Really? I'll be lucky if I could get my mom to show up."

"Oh…"

"Don't worry, I'm just playing around. How are you doing though? It's been a long time. Last time I remember hearing you were dating… one of those business bros…"

"We broke up," Alana interrupted before Brent could remember Paul's name.

She was sure that just hearing his name would send her spiraling into depression.

"Wish I could say I was sorry to hear it," Brent replied with an impish grin.

"Yeah," Alana said coldly.

"Sorry," Brent continued, realizing that he'd made a mistake, "Nasty break up?"

That was the worst part of all of it as far as Alana was concerned. It hadn't been a nasty break up at all. Her feelings for Paul had never had the chance to die. And even now, Alana didn't know how she would respond if she ran into him around campus or around the city. She considered herself lucky that she hadn't seen him around yet.

"It wasn't so much nasty as it was... just not final... You know what I mean?"

Brent nodded.

As Alana looked up at him, she noticed for the first time just how good looking he was. He had a different sort of look than Paul did. He was thick and muscular instead of covered in lean muscle. His cheek bones were sharp and his lips were full and plump. He had a perpetual mischievous look in his eyes and he seemed quiet. At least far quieter than Paul had been.

"I know what you mean," He said, "Listen... If you ever want to work out any of these complicated feelings, call me."

Brent then took a piece of paper from his bag and wrote down his phone number, slipping the piece of paper into Alana's purse. She smiled partly because she liked Brent well enough and partly because she at least had some validation that she was still a hot commodity on the dating market.

"Thanks Brent. I'll let you know if I ever need to take you up on that."

Alana didn't think she would but she at least wanted to be polite. Once he'd made his move, Brent didn't lose interest in talking to her. Alana was glad to have some company. Besides Desiree and her family members, she was so wrapped up in work that she hardly spoke to anyone else. Cute guys were out of the question.

Brent asked, "So you're finishing up in December right? Does it feel good?"

Alana smiled, "It will feel good to be called Dr. Morris finally."

Brent nodded, "Cool. Think you'll stay in Atlanta?"

Alana hadn't thought about it at all. Before, her plan had always been to find work wherever Paul needed to be. He'd be at the helm of his family's insurance company soon enough and he would have had the money to support her career wherever they decided to make roots.

"I might. Is it strange that I haven't thought about it?"

Brent chuckled, "Miss A+ hasn't though about the future? I'm shocked."

"Hey I'm not just a crazy perfectionist! I struggle with things too."

Brent replied, "I doubt that. But you know what Alana, I know that wherever you end up in life, you'll do great."

Before Alana could respond, the secretary called her into the office for her appointment.

"Thanks Brent, I appreciate it. I'll see if I can give you a call some time."

She waved good bye and walked into the office, knowing that Brent was watching her as she walked away from him. When Alana stepped into the registrar's office, the administrator greeted her by name. Apparently, being in the top ten students in your program made your name and face recognizable around campus. Alana didn't even have to do much begging to convince her to get twenty tickets for her family members.

Alana knew that when her family came they'd make a scene. They always did and she loved having her own personal fan club at her graduations. Alana walked out of the office with a smile on her face and as she walked into the hallway, her smile was suddenly wiped away.

Paul. He was walking out of an office in the hall way and a tall, thin looking blonde was following behind him giggling. Alana stopped walking, hoping that without the sound of her shoes against the tiled floors, Paul wouldn't notice her walking alone at the other end of the hallway. She stood still watching his body language with the blonde. Alana was sure they were dating. The girl laughed and flipped her hair behind her ears. Then she tiptoed and kissed Paul on the cheek.

He turned away from her kiss and at that moment, Paul's eyes caught Alana's. When he saw her, she could tell that he wanted to say hello. Alana felt like she'd been stabbed in the gut. She couldn't face Paul like this. She turned around rapidly and tried to take the back exit to the building.

"Alana, wait!"

Her worst nightmare. She could hear Paul's footsteps as he chased after her down the hall. She kept walking, hoping that he'd change his mind and decide not to say a word to her. It had been too long and she didn't want to meet him like this. He was here with another woman and she had no prospects on the horizon unless she wanted something not-so-serious with Brent.

But Alana could't avoid him. Paul tapped her on the shoulder and Alana was forced to turn around and truly face him.

"Alana, don't run away from me."

"Hi Paul," She said flatly, trying desperately not to make eye contact with his bright blue eyes.

"Look at me, please Alana."

Alana hesitantly made eye contact with Paul. A flood of emotions washed over her and she tried to fight back tears. She had known this would be difficult but she couldn't have predicted just how difficult it really would be to see him again.

"You haven't been taking my calls."

"I guess that I've been a bit busy."

"Bullshit Alana."

"Listen Paul, we don't have to do this okay? I can see that you've moved on…"

Paul looked baffled.

"Move on? You think I've moved on from you Alana?"

"Well what am I supposed to think Paul?" Alana replied.

"Listen Alana, whatever you think, you've got it wrong. I've missed you."

Alana bit down on her lip. It wasn't easy for her to hear Paul saying these things. After weeks and weeks apart, no matter how much she was hurting, she knew that she couldn't take him back. She couldn't handle the pain Paul had put her through during their breakup ever again. Giving Paul back his power would mean he could do this to her again. She could be left high and dry with no way to piece herself back together. She wasn't over him, but she was at least willing to stand her ground.

"You shouldn't miss me Paul. I'm fine."

"Well I'm not fine Alana. These past few months without you have been hell."

"I'm sorry to hear that," She said.

Alana was curious but she was trying to hold back as much as possible. She didn't want to give Paul even an inch into her life. Paul still had a way with words and Alana knew that if he wanted to get into her life she wouldn't be able to leave him around.

"Listen Alana, please let's just talk it out together, okay?"

"What do we have to talk about Paul? Really?" Alana said.

"A lot. We have to talk about a lot."

"I can't do this Paul, alright? I really can't take this again. I'm sorry Paul, but you made your choice and now we both have to deal with the repercussions of that choice."

"Don't go like this."

"I'm sorry, I have to."

Alana pushed past Paul and then left the building. Tears welled in her eyes and Alana couldn't hold back any longer. At least she'd managed to hold it together long enough that Paul wouldn't see. It hurt to walk away again, but Alana knew she had to do it. Now their relationship really and truly felt over. There was no going back.

The finality of their relationship felt like it was sinking in on a new level. Alana saw that even if he denied it, Paul was very close to moving on. It was time for her to do the same thing. Even if it would be difficult, Alana would have to pick herself up off the ground and move on. Soon she'd be Dr. Morris. Maybe after that happened it would be time to move out of Atlanta and go somewhere else.

At the very least, the one thing Alana had to look forward to now is that she could go anywhere in the country. She'd have to do it alone but at least she was sure that she could do it.

7 SAVE ME

Accepting the finality of her relationship with Paul meant that Alana had to force herself to go back to living a normal life. She never ended up calling Brent. She wasn't interested in anything casual and she didn't trust herself to have anything with him that had no strings attached. Alana was very much looking for strings to be attached to whatever relationship she pursued.

She wanted strings attached — that was the problem. That was a part of the issue she'd been having with Paul.

Around ten days after she'd run into Paul, Alana's apartment had regained its sparkle. Her graduation was approaching as was Christmas and Thanksgiving. That time of year was Alana's favorite. She loved the smell of pumpkin spice wafting out of coffee shops. She loved the Thanksgiving day drama that happened with her family and all the aunties that came out to celebrate with their broods of cousins.

Alana was the cousin they were all so proud of. Now that she was about to be Dr. Morris, Alana was sure their appreciation for her would climb too.

Alana wanted to give them something to be proud of. So she remained home on a weekend with her thesis and she had been writing day and night. By Saturday evening, Alana was ready to collapse from exhaustion. She'd reviewed her written work over and over again; she was prepared to edit some more before calling it a night.

Alana heard a knock at her door. Strange. She wasn't expecting anyone. The only person she suspected would appear at this hour of the night was Desiree. She'd been known to drag Alana along on her late night shopping sprees.

The person at the door wasn't Desiree. When Alana opened the door, she saw Paul standing there looking quite tense and upset.

"Paul?"

Alana blurted it out as a question because she was in such disbelief that Paul would be the one at her doorstep at a time like this.

"Please let me inside Alana, we need to talk."

"Right now? Paul, it's almost eight at night!"

"Alana," He said, "Please... I'm begging you."

She'd never heard Paul beg before — for anything. Alana had always been soft when it came to Paul but now she was even softer. Even if he'd rubbed her emotions raw, she still cared for him deep down. Now, he looked like he really needed her to care. His beard had grown out and thick stubble covered his chin. There were dark circles underneath his beautiful blue eyes. Alana could tell from his body language that he probably hadn't slept in a while.

She allowed him into her apartment. Paul looked around feverishly as if he expected Alana to be huddled in bed with someone.

"Busy tonight?"

"No Paul, just reading and writing some of my thesis. Are you going to tell me what's wrong?"

Paul's eyes looked glazed over, "Do you have anything to drink?"

"Just some red moscato in the back of my fridge…"

"That'll do."

Perplexed, Alana poured Paul a glass of moscato; she neglected to drink any herself. She led him to her living room and they sat across from each other on Alana's thrifted couches.

"How've you been?"

Alana crossed her legs.

"I've been fine Paul. I'm wondering what's going on with you. You haven't been here since before…" Alana trailed off.

"Since before Martha's Vineyard. I know."

"Well then don't worry about how I've been and spill… What's going on?"

"I've graduated early. I'll still do the ceremony with everyone in January but I'm finished with school and I need to head back to New York."

Alana bit down on her lip. Paul had come here to announce he'd be leaving. If Paul left for New York, the chances were slim that she'd ever see him again. He'd come here to say good-bye. With that realization, Alana felt her heart swell with sadness. Even if their relationship had ended, she still felt attached to Paul in a way she'd never felt about any other man in her past. Paul was special. He'd always been special to her.

"New York?"

"I'm not saying good-bye to you Alana," Paul continued, "I want you to come to New York with me. You're almost done with your thesis. You can fly down here for a couple days a week to tie up your loose ends… But I want you to come up North with me."

"Paul, we're broken up."

Paul looked down and Alana could tell it pained him to be like this and to be so emotionally vulnerable with her. She waited patiently for him to speak up.

"I don't want us to be broken up Alana. I thought I could handle living without you… And I can in a lot of ways. But there are some aspects of my life where you belong and I can't stand the thought of you not being by my side."

Alana wished she could just take Paul back and never look back. She wished that she could grasp his hand in hers and plunge into the future without a care in the world. But that had never been Alana's approach to things and she wasn't about to change now.

"But what about our problems Paul? All those things that tore us apart haven't gone away…"

"I think they have Alana. We just haven't realized it."

"What do you mean Paul?"

"I mean that you've stopped trying to run away Alana. Over the summer, you were willing to stand by me even if you were upset. I hadn't seen that you'd changed. I was the one who broke us apart because to me, changing was the scariest thing in the world."

"How can I trust that things will be different Paul? How can I be so certain that the damage isn't irreparable?"

"Because we still love each other Alana," Paul said, "And don't you dare deny it because you know it's true."

Paul was right. Alana knew that she had no room to deny it either. From the moment she'd received "closure" in the halls of the registrar's office, Alana had been certain that she'd always love Paul no matter what happened between them. She didn't want to admit it. After all the heartbreak she'd been through, admitting that she still loved him would mean being raw, vulnerable, and emotionally weak.

Alana went forward anyways.

"It's true Paul. I... I love you."

"Then come to New York with me."

"When?"

"I don't know... I think we have a few details to work out beforehand."

"Details?" Alana asked, screwing her face up in confusion until she saw the grin breaking out across Paul's face.

"Come on Alana… Don't make me say it out loud."

He stood up and moved over to her, pulling her off the couch. Alana looked into Paul's eyes expecting him to kiss her but uncertain of how it would feel. After all the hurt she'd been through, could it really feel the same? Paul pushed a long coil of Alana's hair out of her face. She searched his eyes for some sense that he felt the same uncertainty.

"Don't be afraid," He whispered.

Then Paul touched his lips to hers. Alana closed her eyes and allowed his warm lips to engulf hers. She kissed back. Alana felt tentative but the longer Paul's lips remained pressed to hers, the more comfortable she felt with him touching her. Paul's hands wandered to her hips and Alana plunged her tongue into his mouth. She wanted him to know that she was ready…

Alana had nearly forgotten that Paul still knew her body intimately. He hadn't forgotten how to pleasure her or turn her on in the slightest.

"Please… Come to bed with me," She whispered. It sounded like begging.

Paul followed her to the bedroom and once she was there, Alana pushed him a few feet away from her and started to undress. She didn't need his dominant command this time. She was pliable to his will without his words; she knew exactly what she wanted and she was still willing to give it to him. It had been months and they had plentiful energy and passion to work out between the two of them.

"You're so gorgeous," Paul whispered as he watched Alana strip her clothes off.

She took of her top and then her cozy yoga pants. Alana stood before him in a matching set of red underwear. (They were her lucky set, coincidentally.) The red stood out against her deep brown skin, highlighting just how beautiful her dark skin was. Color brought out the beauty of those earthy tones. Alana dropped her bra to the ground and then slipped out of her underwear.

Her dark cacao nipples stood perky on her breasts. She removed her underwear and revealed even more to Paul. Her pussy was covered in a thin layer of short hairs. She hadn't expected to see Paul at all… Or to get lucky for a long, long time. Paul didn't seem to mind the natural, unshaven nature to what was between her legs. He was just eager to touch her, to kiss her, and soon make love to her.

He moved over to Alana and started to plant kisses all over her lips and her body. He bent down and let his tongue graze across her bosom. Alana inhaled sharply as she felt his warm tongue against her nipples. She hadn't been subjected to a man's tongue in a long time and she'd underestimated just how sensitive she would be to even his lightest touch.

"I miss your big beautiful tits," Paul grunted as his lips moved to her other breast.

Alana was fully aroused and she could feel her pussy growing more and more moist. Paul took one look at her fully nude and decided what they'd be doing next. He gazed into Alana's eyes and without breaking said gaze, he removed all of his clothing. His cock stood tumescent and proud before him; Alana couldn't help but salivate at the sight of his bulging member. It was huge… Alana knew her mind was playing tricks on her but it was almost bigger than she remembered.

Paul got onto the bed and lay on his back with his dick pointing up to the ceiling.

"Come ride me baby," He said.

Alana moved over to him on the bed and straddled him. Her warm thighs touched his. Paul's hands moved over to her thighs and reached all the way to her buttocks as she positioned her wet pussy right above his waiting hardness. His thick cock would be a tight squeeze but Alana was ready.

She was so caught up in the moment that she hardly had time to process this was really happening. Paul. He was here. They were making love. They were getting back together. She'd be following him to New York. Everything would be okay. Or at least, everything had the chance of being okay.

She used her hands to grasp Paul's cock and place it at the entrance of her pussy. Alana started to lower her hips, allowing Paul's sizable cock head to brush past her entrance ever so slightly. She started to move down his full length slowly. Paul closed his eyes and threw his head back into the pillow in ecstasy. Alana had never seen his face so expressive with pleasure before; she enjoyed watching him like this.

Alana wriggled until Paul's cock was fully embedded in her wetness. She sighed and gasped as she shifted to accommodate the invading member perfectly between her folds. She steadied herself against Paul's rock hard chest and started to move her hips up and down.

Alana started to moan in ecstasy as Paul's dick disappeared deeper and deeper inside her. With each thrust, she found herself getting nearer and nearer to a big climax. Paul gripped her large ass cheeks as she rode him. She could feel his dick stiffening inside her with each stroke. Alana threw her head back and started to thrust harder.

Her long, natural hair almost touched his chest when she threw her head back. Her beautiful, thick coils of pure black hair looked almost like a giant halo around her head as she rode him. Paul grunted as he watched Alana bouncing on his dick. Her large breasts undulated with each thrust. Her ass cheeks jiggled with each motion. Soon, Alana couldn't hold back. She cried out as she climaxed.

Her pussy grew slick with her juices and she shuddered as she climaxed.

"Yes! Yes Paul! Oh God!"She pleaded as she climaxed.

Paul held her steadied and continued to assist her hips moving up and down his cock, even as she grew weaker and weaker with her climax. Paul lifted Alana off his cock once he felt her quivering turn into trembling pleasure.

"Get on all fours baby," He grunted.

Alana obeyed. She got on all fours and arched her back magnificently, exposing her pussy and asshole to Paul. He placed a thumb against her backdoor and then lined his dick up with her wetness. Alana pushed her hips back, engulfing his entire dick inside her pussy.

She cried out loudly as Paul slid his full length inside her.

"Oh!"

"Like that baby?"

"Yes! Please... Fuck me harder Paul! Harder!"

Paul obliged her pleas. Alana craved another climax even more powerful than the last. Paul gripped her ass cheeks, spread them apart and then started to hammer his powerful cock between her moistened folds. The sensation of Paul's cock ramming deep inside her and then grazing along her sensitive outer folds pushed Alana over the edge again.

Another climax wracked over her body causing her to lose her balance. She lay on her tummy, clutching one of her pillows, with just her ass sticking up into the air. Paul held her hips still and continued to drive his cock between her slick pussy lips. The tightness of the position brought him closer and closer to a big release of his own.

Alana thrust her hips back as much as she could, forcing Paul's dick to drive deeper and deeper inside her. Paul let out an animalistic groan and Alana knew he was getting closer. Two or three more thrusts later, Paul's dick twitched powerfully. Cum erupted from his dick forcefully. Alana lay still as Paul coated the walls of her pussy with spurts of his juices. She knew that this was wrong...and risky... But it felt oh-so-good.

Paul removed his dick from between her lips. She was shuddering in total ecstasy. Paul's dick was covered in her juices. They both rolled over onto their backs. Their hands snaked across the bedsheets towards each other until their pinky fingers locked. They were together again and somehow, despite everything, it felt so-so right. Alana exhaled in relief — somehow, she'd landed a second chance with Paul.

Paul looked over at Alana, shocked and surprised that this woman had dared to take him back. Paul had figured all hope was lost but he couldn't let Alana go. He knew he had to be willing to fight for her. And he had fought for her... The reward had been ever so sweet.

As they lay in bed together, Alana felt a mixture of relief and worry. If this was really it between them, if they were back together again, what did that really mean? If she followed Paul to New York, what would she be leaving behind?

Paul looked over at Alana and noticed how lost in thought she was. He grabbed one of her coils and pulled gently.

"What's up?" Paul asked.

"Hm?" Alana snapped out of her trance, "I was just lost in thought I suppose."

"Must have been some crazy thought. You looked practically hypnotized."

Alana smiled, "It's not that. I'm just happy you're here Paul. But also, I can't help but worry."

"Worry?"

"I don't want us to go through this again."

Paul kissed her cheek, "I don't want us to go through this again either."

"How can I be sure Paul?"

"You have to be sure that I love you at least?"

Alana nodded. That she knew. Ironically, Paul wouldn't have said anything to her if he hadn't loved her. As much as their breakup had hurt, she at least understood a part of Paul's perspective on the matter. He hadn't done because he wanted to hurt her, but because he wanted to stop.

"I know you love me."

"Listen Alana in the past few months, I've replayed every word you said to me over and over again. I thought about all the ways you tried to tell me that you felt out of place in my world. Because I didn't know what to say, I thought I could ignore the problem and it would go away."

"And you've changed?"

Paul chuckled, "Changed? Hell yeah I've changed. I finally figured out Alana that I can't just ignore all of this stuff. It's your every day isn't it. I've been reading more and trying to learn about all this racism stuff. I don't want our skin color to be a barrier between us Alana."

Alana looked over at him and saw that he was serious. She was so enamored with Paul in that moment that she wanted to make love to him all over again.

"I love you Paul."

Paul replied assuredly, "I love you too."

Alana sat up and moved down to his waist. Even if Paul had just released inside her, she was sure that she could coax more pleasure out of him with just a little bit of effort. Her hands grabbed Paul's soft dick and she started to glide her hands up and down the length of his member. Paul's dick started to grow thicker in her hands. He let out a loud exhalation, letting Alana know that he was settling into things.

With alarmingly few strokes, Paul's dick was rock hard. Thick veins climbed up the sides of his cock and it had been pumped full with blood and raw desire for Alana. She bent her head to his dick and took just the head into her mouth. Paul shuddered as she wrapped her plump lips around his large dick head. She applied tight suction around his head and then flicked her tongue around the sensitive opening.

Paul's dick twitched in her mouth. She teased the tip a bit longer until Paul thrust his hips up desperately into her mouth. He gasped when Alana took his full length deep into her mouth. Paul groaned as the tip of his cock grazed the back of Alana's throat. She loved the feeling of his blood filled hard cock touching the back of her throat and filling her up. Given the choice between breathing and taking in more of Paul, she would always choose swallowing Paul's cock.

She started to slide his length in and out of her mouth slowly. She could tell that each delicate motion of her tongue brought Paul closer and closer to climax. Even if he'd already finished once, he was hardly spent. He still wanted to cum again; he could still fill Alana up with another thick load of his seed.

"Deeper," He commanded.

Alana thrust his dick deeper than before, almost choking on his thickness. Paul thrust his hips up and Alana began to bob her head relentlessly. Paul was too consumed by pleasure to take control again. He let out soft masculine groans as Alana plunged him further and further down her throat.

"Yes babe… Yes…"

Alana took her mouth off Paul's dick for a moment and began to use her hands to keep him hard. She closed her palms around his thick staff and glided her hands up and down the slippery length as fast as possible. Alana bent her head to Paul's velvety sack and began to slide her tongue along his balls. Paul groaned loudly this time as she took one testicle into her mouth and rolled it around. She moved her lips to the other one and felt Paul's dick stiffen in her hand. He was close… She knew it.

Alana removed her hand from Paul's dick and kept her mouth firmly planted around his balls. Paul couldn't stand it much longer. He tapped Alana on the shoulder and guided her onto her back. Paul pushed Alana's legs up into the air and took a glimpse of her soft, wet pussy.

She was glistening with her juices and Paul could tell that her swollen pussy was ready for another hard pounding. Before thrusting his hard dick inside her, Paul bent his lips between her thighs. Alana gasped as Paul started to rub his tongue along the length of her slit furiously.

"Oh! Oh! Oh!" Alana gasped at the top of her lungs.

She was sure that all the neighbors in her apartment building could hear every single sound she was making. Paul pushed her legs back further and thrust his tongue deep between her folds. Paul passionately wrapped his lips around Alana's clit and french kissed her extra-sensitive nub.

Alana couldn't avoid climax this time. As Paul's tongue flicked back and forth furiously, she cried out.

"Yes! I'm cumming Paul! I'm cumming!"

Her screams of pleasure only encouraged Paul to use his tongue more. He nibbled at her outer lips until she was close to climax again. Paul slid two of his fingers between her folds and Alana cried out again. Paul kept his lips fastened around her nub and began to probe her deeply with his two fingers. She gasped and cried out as she came again.

Paul's fingers rubbed against her g-spot and drove Alana to yet another climax. Her hair was a disheveled mess and she gasped desperately for breath. This incredible romp had her covered in sweat and the juices from her sex. When Paul pulled his face away from her wetness, Alana didn't just want him between her thighs. She needed him.

"I'm going to fuck you so hard," He said.

Alana nodded. Hell, it was exactly what she wanted. She wanted to feel that peace she'd felt when Paul had used her for his own pleasure. She wanted to feel the comfort of submission and the mixture of fear and excitement that came with getting a good hard pummeling from Paul.

He lined his dick up with Alana's moist entrance and slid all the way in with one thrust.

"Yes!" Alana groaned as he slid inside her.

She gripped Paul's ass cheeks, digging her nails into his muscular ass and pulling him in deeper. Paul let out a loud animalistic grunt and then began thrusting into Alana's wetness with immense force. This type of hard pounding was so deliciously taboo. Paul's face contorted as he rammed into her harder and deeper. He grabbed Alana's hands and pinned them above her head.

She lay there, utterly exposed and vulnerable to Paul's most twisted desires. He pushed her legs back so far that Alana thought they were going to break. In this angle, Paul's hardness grazed against the most sensitive and untouched parts of Alana's pussy. She continued to gasp and wriggled beneath Paul's hard thrusting.

"Harder," She egged him on.

Paul pounded her even harder and she screamed out in another climax. Her mind exploded into a million pieces and all she could do was lie there and feel every single sensation that Paul delivered to her. She was in love with him and she was in love with every little thing he did to bring her pleasure.

Alana was certain that Paul was going to release soon. She held his cheek and looked deep into his eyes as he plunged into her. Yes, they'd made the right choice getting back together. They'd both changed in so many ways, yet they both also wanted exactly the same things.

Paul closed his eyes and groaned as he released inside Alana again. And again, she knew the risks but she continued to take them. With Paul, somehow risks all felt less risky. After he pulled out of her, they lay by each other's side again. This all felt so good. So perfectly blissful.

Alana and Paul fell asleep in each other's arms. They stayed asleep for hours until their night was interrupted by the ringing of Paul's cellphone. Alana woke up confused by the noise. She reached on her bedside table for her phone before she realized it was Paul's. Alana nudged him until he woke up.

Paul answered the call while Alana checked the time. It was three in the morning.

"Hello?" Paul rasped groggily.

He was quiet for a while. Alana couldn't hear much of what was happening at the other end of the line but she could tell it was Paul's mother, Charlotte. She could also tell that Charlotte sounded frenetic.

"We'll get the next flight out of Atlanta."

Paul hung up and buried his head in his hands. Alana rested her hand on his thighs and tried to wake herself up. A call at three in the morning rarely ever meant good news.

"Alana, I'll need to fly up to New York tomorrow," He said morosely.

"Tomorrow?" Alana exclaimed, "What's wrong Paul? Is everything okay?"

Alana was starting to wonder if something was seriously wrong, something Paul hadn't been telling her.

"My father had a heart attack tonight," Paul said slowly after a long period of silence.

Alana's mouth dropped open but she still didn't know how to respond, or what to say. Was there anything she could say?

Paul continued, "Could I borrow your computer so I can book a flight out of here tomorrow morning please?"

Alana nodded, "Sure… But Paul, I think I should come with you."

Alana walked over to her desk and grabbed her computer, setting it down on the bed next to Paul. He looked up at her as if he wasn't sure her offer was sincere.

"Are you sure Alana? This won't be a vacation or anything."

"So what?" Alana replied, "I'm not with you because I think everything's going to be a vacation Paul. If you don't know what's going on with your father or if it's something serious, I want to be by your side."

Paul let a light smirk slip, "Let me guess. You won't take no for an answer?"

Alana smiled back at him, "I don't think we should abandon each other Paul. If we want to be together for a long time, not everything's going to be easy."

"What about work? School?"

"I have no classes tomorrow and I can cancel all my work engagements."

Paul opened up Alana's computer and started to book flights. The earliest flight they could find out of Atlanta left at eight in the morning the next day. Looking at the time, Alana realized that there would be absolutely no time for sleep. Paul booked a three night stay for them and they'd both have to pack.

"Are you sure you want to go up there with me?" Paul asked.

Alana nodded, "I'm sure Paul. I want you to know... I'm going to be by your side no matter what."

Paul grabbed Alana's hand and kissed it.

"Thanks Alana," He said.

They hopped out of bed and Alana immediately put on her coffee maker. If she was going to be up at three, she needed a little something extra to get herself going. She noticed that Paul seemed upset, but he didn't exactly seem devastated that Paul Hanover II had gone into cardiac arrest. Alana didn't know what to make of it.

She'd always suspected that Paul had a difficult relationship with his father but she'd been too polite to ever ask him about the nature of their relationship. While drinking her coffee and getting together a nice weekend bag, she watched Paul fuss about being separated from clothes of his own.

"I think I still have some old t-shirts of yours…" Alana admitted.

"Yeah?"

"They're in a shoe box in the back of my closet."

Maybe she hadn't been as close to getting over Paul as she thought if she was keeping his old clothes. Alana had just never been able to bear the thought of getting rid of them. Paul reached for the shoe box and Alana tossed the shirts he'd procured from them into her duffel.

Paul sighed and then spoke, "I bet you find my reaction to all this pretty strange, huh?"

"Strange?" Alana asked, worried that she'd betrayed her own emotions.

"It's fine. It is strange. My father and I have always been very similar but never close. He was always so busy with the company that he never made much time for me when I was a kid. He's doing better with Cosima but to me, he's always just been some stranger. He only really started to give a damn about me when I told him I'd go get an MBA…"

Paul paused for a moment then continued, "He's been a big drinker for years and it's been slowing him down. I noticed that and of course, I thought I could help and be the family savior by getting this MBA. The thing is Alana… I don't have a damned clue what I'm doing. I just hope nothing happens to the guy before I'm ready…"

Tears welled in Paul's eyes but he pushed them to the background. Alana walked up to him and kissed him on the cheek.

"You're so strong, my love," She whispered into his ears.

And she meant it. Alana knew the circumstances of their Northern travels were less than desirable. The only comfort she had was knowing that she was making the right choice by staying by Paul's side no matter what.

8 INHERITANCE

The flight up to New York had a somber tone. Alana
held onto Paul's hand as they sat in their first class
seats. Neither of them did very much talking. Alana
rested her head on Paul's arm and closed her eyes. The
past twenty-four hours hadn't exactly played out like
she'd expected them to. This was all surreal. She was
glad to be back in Paul's arms and to feel more secure
than she'd ever felt with him.

Still, Alana couldn't help but worry that everything
wouldn't be alright for long. She remembered how
things had been the last time she met the Hanover
family. They weren't exactly the most pleasant bunch
of people to be around. Alana couldn't help but worry
that under the duress of Paul Hanover II's illness,
things would be even worse.

Plus, Alana worried about Paul too. He seemed like he
was handling everything in stride but it couldn't
exactly be easy to "handle" the thought of losing your
father. Paul claimed that he wasn't close to his
namesake but to Alana, that made this even worse. If
anything happened to Paul Hanover II, they'd never be
close to each other. Alana didn't want Paul to lose out
on a valuable relationship with his father.

They arrived in New York and breezed out through the arrivals gate onto the street. Alana had been all over the South but she'd never been to New York City before.

"Let's look for my family's car," Paul directed her.

Alana had no idea what to look for. Eventually she saw a black Lincoln town car with a short, tanned looking man holding a sign saying "Hanover". She pointed it out to Paul and they made their way to the car. The driver took their bags and gave Paul a big hug.

"How ya doin'?" He asked Paul in a thick Brooklyn accent.

"Not so bad Sergei. Worried about my father."

Sergei nodded, "I understand. Hospital first?"

Paul nodded. Sergei held open the door in the back seat and allowed both Alana and Paul to slide in. Once they slid into the back, Paul slid up the partition between the two of them.

"Sergei understands that I always like a bit of privacy after I travel," Paul told her.

Alana squeezed Paul's hand tightly.

"So we're headed to the hospital?" She asked.

Paul said, "Yes, last I heard from my mother they were at Mount Sinai. I guess I'm just hoping they've discharged him already."

Alana could tell that Paul was scared, even if he didn't say anything to really shower it. He'd brought her here, all the way up north because he couldn't handle the possibility that anything happened to his father alone.

They got to Mount Sinai and walked in through the large double doors to the reception area. Paul found a proper looking nurse and he got her attention.

"Good morning ma'am," He said, "I'm Paul Hanover… I think my father is in one of your wards and I want to know if I can visit him…"

"Oh you made it!" She said, "Follow me."

Paul and Alana exchanged glances. What on earth did that mean? They followed the nurse through a long hallway, up five floors in the elevator and then down another long hallway.

"Your family is in a private waiting room with the doctor. I'll let you talk to them first…"

Alana looked the woman up and down and noted the overly sympathetic look in her eye. Alana got chills. Paul didn't seem to be as suspicious but Alana was starting to feel very odd about this; she suspected that something was very wrong with her boyfriend's father.

Paul pushed open the door to enter the waiting room and came upon everyone in his family crying. The doctor stood in front of them. Charlotte and Cosima were holding onto each other tightly. Paul's grandmother stood there with an agitated look on her face and silent tears streaming down it.

The doctor looked to Paul as if to ask him "Who the hell are you?"

"Hi, Doctor... I'm Paul Hanover. Uh... Paul Hanover's son," He said.

The doctor nodded, "You might want to sit down Paul..."

Chills broke out over Alana's body and a lump formed in her throat preemptively. It could only be one thing.

Paul sat down and the doctor started talking. Everything started to feel even more surreal. The doctor told Paul in excruciating detail what had happened. Paul Hanover II had gone into cardiac arrest. They took him to the hospital and he went into cardiac arrest after he'd been stabilized. There was nothing they could do about it: Paul Hanover II was dead.

Paul didn't say anything for a while. He stood up and shook the doctor's hand answering, "Thank you Doctor."

Alana could tell that he was holding back until the doctor left. Paul seemed detached from his body, almost as if he hadn't realized what was happening. His mother reached for his hand. For the first time, Alana saw a truly tender moment between mother and son.

"I need to see him," Paul said quietly.

Cosima held her brother's hand and they walked towards the door where their father lay. Charlotte walked up to Alana and whispered, "Thank you for being here for him dear."

It was the nicest things that any of the Hanovers had ever said to Alana. Paul and Cosima entered the room where their dead father lay and Alana heard their sobs growing louder and louder. Alana's eyes welled up as she thought of the grief that Paul must be going through. Losing his father couldn't be easy, even if they weren't very close.

After a long spell in his father's room, Paul and Cosima finally emerged. The rest of the day breezed by unhappily. There were details to attend to and Paul had to be in charge of all of it. Alana mostly spent the time chatting and having tea with Cosima and Charlotte who were both determined to still be the perfect hosts. Even Paul's grandmother was on her best behavior.

Over the next few days, Paul realized that there was no way he could return to the south after this. Alana knew that she should stay by his side so she tried to work out how she could orchestrate this move up North.

Paul Hanover II was buried exactly ten days after he passed away. From the day he died, Paul Hanover III had to start running the family's insurance company. That meant Alana had to be in charge of a million little details all at once. She flew South and hired moving companies to pack up both her apartment and Paul's for the move to New York City. She got them a nice, comfortable Midtown apartment with one of the best views in the city.

As all this was happening, Alana also found herself getting closer to Charlotte Hanover. At first, Alana had found Charlotte almost terrifyingly cold. In the wake of her husband's death, Charlotte had found an impetus to start trusting Alana. Seeing how Alana remained so utterly dedicated to Paul, she realized that the girl had to be there for more than the Hanover fortune. Her walls slipped down a bit and Alana began to feel like she was really a part of the family.

They moved to midtown and Alana started to look for work in her field. Her PhD was almost finished and her advisors were utterly understanding of her situation. Alana spent her days running errands related to home management and sending out job applications by the bundle. It was all very stressful but nothing she experienced was as bad as the duress that Paul was under.

Taking over the helm of a company suddenly meant Paul was working 12 hour days, every single day. They hardly saw each other and when they did, Paul barely had energy to do a thing. He was still grieving his father but he couldn't show that grief, not even a little bit when he stepped into board meetings or executive offices. Paul had the daunting task of convincing people that the former CEO's young son wouldn't run the company into the ground.

Alana couldn't wait for the pressure to die down. She loved Paul, but their relationship had only been recently mended. They were still at risk of things falling apart, especially with this increased stress in their lives. Alana was starting to worry.

After a few more days, Alana was convinced that her worry was starting to make her ill. She woke up feeling terribly nauseous and just *sick.* She hadn't gotten this ill since before her graduate school entrance exams. That level of stress had been unbelievable but academic stress had nothing on the real life stressors of the outside world.

When Alana's morning nausea didn't disappear after a week, she started to worry that this had nothing to do with stress. Her period was a few days late according to her calendar. Alana knew that she'd been less than responsible with Paul, but the timing of this was far more inconvenient than even she had predicted. Alana knew that she'd have to get around to telling Paul the truth — there was a good chance she was carrying his child.

With Paul working 12 hour days, five days a week, Alana knew she'd have to wait 'til the weekend to tell him. With the realization that she was pregnant, Alana slowed down on her job search and instead turned her attention to her PhD work. Given the circumstances, she'd been given special permission to finish up by correspondence.

When the weekend rolled around, Paul insisted that they have a Saturday morning brunch together in this little indoor park area that overlooked Central Park. It was the perfect winter alternative to Central Park. Alana wished that she could have announced this news to him in the comfort of their apartment, but Paul was *insistent* that they have brunch in over there, so she agreed. Alana hadn't had time to see much of the city outside of her errands, so she relished the idea of seeing one of the most iconic scenes in New York.

She packed up some orange juice and champagne along with finger sandwiches and a cheese plate. With access to the finest food in New York as well as Paul's credit card, Alana found herself exploring the most gourmet choices for food. Alana had been up for a few hours on Saturday when Paul wandered out of their bedroom. He carried the exhaustion of grief and a taxing job on his face.

"Good morning babe," He mumbled, making his way behind Alana and then kissing her on the cheek.

"Good morning," She answered, turning around and wrapping Paul up in a big hug.

Alana asked, "How do you feel?"

"Hm… Tired," Paul said, planting a kiss on Alana's forehead, "And hungry."

Alana chuckled.

"Well, everything is ready for us to head out. Why don't you take a shower and we can leave?"

Paul nodded and walked off to the shower slowly. Alone again, Alana rehearsed the speech she planned to give him over and over in her head. She'd have to open slowly and remind Paul how much she loved him. Then she'd just casually mention that she thought she was pregnant and see how he reacted. Alana knew her anxiety was silly. Paul had always expressed the desire to have a child, especially with her. The timing just seemed so wrong that the whole issue had manufactured heavy anxiety within Alana that she wasn't sure she could really shake.

She heard the shower go on and she took a few deep breaths before finishing packing up the picnic and calling Sergei to meet them in the car within fifteen minutes. Alana mused at how quickly she'd adapted to this life in comparison to Martha's Vineyard. Given the pressure they both were under, she didn't have the option to *not* adapt. Plus, New York City was a touch more diverse than Martha's Vineyard. At least while she was out on the streets, Alana didn't feel much like an outsider.

Paul got out of the shower and got dressed. Alana marveled at how great he looked. He wore a blue checkered button down that highlighted the gorgeous blue in his eyes and then a pair of khaki pants. Alana wasn't used to the chilly New York weather so she wore a black Cashmere turtleneck, black leather leggings and black boots. Alana's natural hair was suffering in the chilly weather, so she wore a knit cap with a silk lining to protect her sensitive strands.

"Ready?" Paul asked.

Alana nodded and pointed to the picnic basket.

"I've been working on this all morning and I called Sergei to come over and get us."

"Perfect, just let me get my coat then," Paul replied with a smile.

They got their coats and gloves then carried their picnic basket to the building's entrance where Sergei was waiting patiently in the cold.

"Very cold today miss!" He said to Alana.

She was still getting used to the heavy New York accents that were so heavy in juxtaposition to the lilting Southern accents she was used to. They got into the backseat of the car then drove to the building with the gorgeous indoor park Paul had raved about. They took the elevator up and Alana found herself in some of the most beautiful botanical gardens she'd ever seen. Paul seemed utterly familiar with the place and he led Alana to a giant window that overlooked Central Park.

Alana was blown away. Paul wouldn't let her keep staring for long or she could have spent hours watching the little people walking through the park and the city streets. Alana couldn't begin to imagine how lush Central Park would be in the summer or even in the autumn. Paul led her to a somewhat isolated picnic table where a familiar scent wafted over to her.

"What's the smell?"

"They grow peonies up here I think. I wanted to take you somewhere that reminded you of home," Paul said, giving Alana a kiss.

His warm lips were especially welcome given the cold weather surrounding them outside. Alana took off her coat but Paul stood there, still wearing his, just watching her.

"Paul?" Alana asked, "Are we going to eat?"

Paul just smiled at her for a moment and then he dropped down on one knee, pulling a little box out of his coat pocket. Alana's hands clasped over her mouth. She'd had big news for Paul so she hadn't even noticed all the little signs that he'd been up to something himself. Paul opened the little box and Alana let out a loud shriek.

"Paul!"

"Wait, Alana, let me speak first," He said.

Alana nodded and tried to push the tears of joy out of her eyes.

"I've always known that we belonged together Alana. We've been through so much and I haven't always been the man that you've needed me to be. While your skin color hasn't been a barrier to me loving you, it's impacted everything in your life and it took me too long to understand that... Meanwhile, even if you've been impulsive and cautious with me, you've always stood by my side no matter what. Now, this might seem like a strange time to propose but now I know that without a doubt, you'll be by my side no matter what. I want to prove to you I'll do the same... Will you marry me Alana?"

"YES!" Alana yelled.

Paul smiled widely and Alana held her hands out so he could slip the magnificent ring on her finger. The ring truly was magnificent in every single way. Four giant diamonds on a gold band that fit Alana's ring finger perfectly. Once the ring had been fit snugly on her fingers, she pulled Paul off his feet and he kissed her long and hard.

"I love you Alana."

"I love you too…"

Once they pulled apart from each other, Alana couldn't bear to spill her secret next. She wanted to enjoy their morning brunch and this rare moment of utter celebration. Despite losing his father, Paul managed to still be thinking about them and their future together. That meant something.

"Christmas is coming up," Paul said, "That means we'll have to have… A spring wedding?"

Alana nodded.

A spring wedding sounded nice but she wasn't sure if she'd be able to handle everything associated with wedding planning if she was carrying a child. Since she was really starting to think she was pregnant, Alana cleverly avoided actually *drinking* any mimosas. She had orange juice on its own and allowed Paul to enjoy their Moët for both of them. After a few mimosas, he was all over her.

Their new engagement meant that there was a small glimmer of light amidst his stress and anxiety. They finished up their brunch and then met Sergei for a ride home. Once they got into their apartment, Alana still didn't get a chance to spill the beans to Paul. He was excited — thrilled even — and he couldn't keep his hands off Alana.

Once they were in their apartment he hugged her and said, "Mrs. Dr. Hanover, how do you like that?"

Alana liked it. *A lot.* Now that she'd had a real and proper taste of what her life with Paul could hold, she was starting to get used to it. New York City promised a very different life than the life of Martha's Vineyard, or Atlanta. Alana liked it up here. She also loved the way that being in Paul's world meant that she was *never* stressed about money. Alana never expected a man to take care of her, but with Paul, she at least felt like it was a possibility that money would never be an issue between the two of them.

"Why don't we take things up to the bedroom Mrs. Hanover?" He asked.

Alana was happy to oblige. Love-making had been reduced to a bare minimum since Paul II's passing. Once they were in their bedroom together, Paul couldn't keep his hands off Alana. He slipped her out of her turtleneck and then out of her pants until she was in just her underwear. Their house was cool, but not cold and Alana's nipples perked up through her bra.

Paul grazed her nipples with his tongue through her bra and Alana shuddered in pleasure. Paul slid her out of her underwear and then carried her onto their bed. Alana got onto all fours expectantly, exposing her ass and pussy to Paul.

"Condom?" He asked.

Alana didn't have the heart to tell him *then* that it didn't matter so she agreed to use one. She heard Paul strip to nothing and then slip a condom over his member. She breathed in deeply. Things had happened fast but she was still fantastically aroused. Paul's scent filled the room and there was the further arousal that came from the fact that they were finally going to take their relationship to the next level.

"Beg for it Mrs. Hanover," Paul demanded.

Alana wriggled her ass cheeks in delight. She loved when Paul allowed their love-making to take a kinky turn like this.

"Please give it to me…"

"Uh uh… Ask properly."

"Please give it to me Mr. Hanover."

"What do you want?"

"Fuck me."

"Fuck you?"

"Please fuck me with your big hard dick Mr. Hanover."

"That's more like it."

Paul eased behind her on the bed but he didn't thrust his dick in all at once. First, Paul bent his head between Alana's thighs and started to lap at her pussy to get it nice and wet. The heat from Paul's tongue contrasted nicely with the cool weather in their bedroom. Alana shuddered and arched her back further to meet his probing tongue.

"Yes…" She moaned softly.

Paul gripped both her thighs and then started to lick at her folds more furiously. From this angle his nose was practically buried between Alana's ass cheeks as he thrust his tongue deeper and deeper along her slit. Paul began to feverishly lap at her slit allowing his teeth to gently graze her outer folds.

Alana began to make soft mewling noises of pleasure. Paul slowed down the pace to tease her with his invasive tongue. He started at her clit and then allowed his tongue to drag slowly along the length of her wetness. Alana quivered in pleasure and as a climax started to build in her core. In this position, she was starting to crave Paul's dick between her legs or in her more taboo area…

Paul showed no signs of letting up his tongue's assault on her pussy. Alana thrust her hips back to meet his eager licks as she came. She cried out and gripped the bedsheets as juices leaked out of her wet pussy. Paul didn't seem deterred by her release and he kept slurping up her juices and tickling her nub over and over again until she came once more.

By this point, Alana was desperate to beg Paul to make love to her a second time.

"Please…"

"No… Take it," He asserted.

He was going to take things at his own pace and there was nothing she could do to convince him otherwise. Paul added his fingers into the mix and inserted two fingers gingerly between Alana's folds. They slipped into her pussy easily and she gasped out in pleasure again. Paul began to thrust his fingers into her pussy, simulating the erotic action of his massive cock.

His fingers grazed Alana's g-spot and delivered unspeakable pleasure throughout her entire body. Alana moaned out in pleasure again as another climax surged through her body. As Paul's fingers started to move in and out of her pussy magnificently, his tongue focused on the back end of her pussy and even slipped to her most forbidden hole.

As Paul's tongue plunged around Alana's most forbidden hole she felt a new sort of pleasure surging through her body. The pleasure associated with the taboo and his tongue flicking across the most sensitive skin on her body drove her wild again. She couldn't wait to feel Paul's giant dick sliding in and out of her pussy folds and rubbing up against her outer lips with each thrust.

"More…" Alana begged.

"More?"

"I need… your… dick," She gasped.

Paul got an impish look on his face that Alana saw when she turned around.

"Oh, you'll get my dick alright."

Paul started to work Alana's ass with his thumb. His large thumb slipped through her tight sphincter first. Alana felt the beginnings of forbidden pleasure convulsing through her pussy as Paul began to ram his thumb deeper and deeper into her backdoor.

Her pussy grew wetter with each thrust and she had the daring fantasy of getting filled in both holes at once…

It was almost like Paul could read her mind. He pulled his thumb out of Alana's ass and gestured towards her bedside table.

"Get your little toy out of there," He growled.

Yes… Alana couldn't wait for her kinkiest fantasies to be fulfilled. Allowing Paul to unleash his dominance had unlocked submissiveness she'd tried to bury beneath the surface for most of her life. In the bedroom with Paul, she was liberated to try everything her heart desired. Her husband understood her better than anybody and he was willing to use her body exactly the way she wanted to be used.

While Alana was grabbing her toy, Paul moved to his own bedside and pulled out a pair of fluffy handcuffs. While she was on all fours, he cuffed Alana's hands together behind her back. In this ultra-submissive position, Paul started to use lube on Alana's asshole and pussy. She was covered in tingling oils that engorged her pussy even further. The slightest touch would drive her wild…

Paul then started to use Alana's toy on her asshole. First he tantalized the area around her backdoor. She shuddered and shivered as she waited for him to ram it in. Paul didn't ram it in quickly though. He worked slowly, building up Alana's desire to get fucked in the ass. He slipped the thick pink toy just past her sphincter. Alana shuddered and he watched her pussy lips twitch in desire… She was enjoying this…

Paul thrust one of his fingers deep into Alana's wetness and as she cried out, he worked the toy into her ass a few inches, causing her to cry out again. Her ass was now full to capacity and adjusting to the new invader. Alana moaned as Paul started to work the toy in and out of her tight asshole. Alana quivered and convulsed after a few short moments in climax.

"Yes!! Yes Paul!" She cooed.

Something about this turned her on in unbelievable ways. She craved every minute of this and more... She wanted it harder. She wanted it hotter. She needed Paul to use all her holes magnificently.

With the toy firmly buried in her asshole, Paul lined his sheathed cock up with her pussy. He plunged into Alana's pussy in one swift motion causing her to scream out in a mixture of surprise and pure ecstasy. Now, she had a sex toy buried in her asshole and Paul's dick stretching out her pussy. There was not one erogenous zone down there that wasn't being subjected to incredible amounts of stimulation.

Unable to hold back any longer, Paul started thrusting into Alana's wetness, moving the toy out at a much slower pace. The mixture of sensations drove Alana crazy. Her juices spurted out of her pussy, sheathing Paul's dick in a thick layer of creamy euphoria. He started to plunge his dick even harder into her, grunting with each animalistic thrust.

With her ass and pussy both being stretched to capacity and her arms decommissioned, all Alana could do was stay there and cum over and over again. She climaxed so many times that she lost track. Paul eventually pulled the sex toy out of her ass when she was screaming so loudly, he thought she would faint from the pleasure.

Now, with just her fiancé's bulging cock buried in her pussy, Alana's orgasms were less intense but more focused. She came a few more times as Paul began to thrust harder and faster. A thin layer of sweat pooled all over his perfect body and he gripped Alana's ass cheeks tightly. She convulsed in pleasure as she felt Paul getting closer to a finish of his own.

Paul grunted magnificently and then came. He groaned for a few moments and then remained embedded inside Alana to catch his breath. They were both utterly spent by the time Paul removed his cock from between Alana's soft, sopping pussy lips. Once he rolled the condom off, he released Alana from her binds. He had expected her to be tired or exhausted but their intense romp had left Alana with a surprisingly energized look on her face.

"Shower?" Paul asked.

Alana nodded. Once they were in the shower together, she was tempted to ask Paul to bend her over and take her again. But she held herself back. She still had to tell Paul the news she'd been hiding from him. They'd been distracted enough and it was already almost mid afternoon. They soaped each other down in the shower instead. Paul helped Alana condition and detangle her long natural strands with his fingers. The intimate act of letting Paul touch her natural hair felt just as good as making love to Alana. For her, hair always meant something intimate and special.

Once they were out of the shower and dressed, Paul still couldn't take his eyes off her.

"That was incredible Alana."

"I know…"

"Is this what we have to look forward to our entire lives?"

Alana thought to herself that they had to look forward to that and more. With a baby on the way, their lives were about to get more hectic, more beautiful, more of everything…

"I think we have that and more to look forward to," She finally said out loud.

Paul looked confused.

"Paul, I've been meaning to tell you something too."

"What is it Alana?"

"I'm pregnant."

"Are you sure?!"

"No, I'm not sure… But I'm almost sure. My period's late and I've been getting really nauseous…"

"Come here," He demanded.

Alana walked close to him and he wrapped his arms around her, kissing her on the lips again.

"I'm so happy with you Alana…"

"So this isn't bad timing?"

"Who gives a damn about the timing? Our family, our lives… There's never a bad time for any of it because we get to write our own story."

"You're right…"

"There's only one thing I have to ask," Paul started.

"What is it?"

"I'm not sure if it's just all that's happened or if I really want this. But if he's a boy, can we name him Paul?"

"Paul Hanover IV?"

"Yes."

Alana had never considered that she'd be carrying on the generational tradition in Paul's family. But given all that had happened between them she was more willing than ever to oblige Paul's wishes. Now, she was going to be a Hanover. That meant she was a part of Paul's family. Given the fact that Paul had lost his father and that she loved him more than anything, she felt destined to agree.

"Of course we can Paul!"

"But… What if it's a girl?" She asked.

Paul grinned, "Then you get to choose her name… Fair's fair."

"Well aren't I a lucky girl…"

"And I'm the luckiest man in the world to have you by my side," Paul whispered.

Alana tiptoed up to his lips and kissed him one more time. She couldn't wait for them to start their lives together.

THE END.

If you enjoyed this story, please visit www.jamilajasperromance.com for a chance to join Jamila Jasper's mailing list and win three free ebooks in the process.

Made in the USA
Monee, IL
10 April 2022

94470077R00142